Arlie,

Best wishes. I hope you enjoy this book about a fellow hunter.

Colter's West Wind

CHRISTOPHER B. HODGES

Copyright © 2017 Christopher B. Hodges.

All rights reserved. No part of this book may be reproduced, stored, or transmitted by any means—whether auditory, graphic, mechanical, or electronic—without written permission of the author, except in the case of brief excerpts used in critical articles and reviews. Unauthorized reproduction of any part of this work is illegal and is punishable by law.

ISBN: 978-1-4834-7275-1 (sc)
ISBN: 978-1-4834-7276-8 (e)

Because of the dynamic nature of the Internet, any web addresses or links contained in this book may have changed since publication and may no longer be valid. The views expressed in this work are solely those of the author and do not necessarily reflect the views of the publisher, and the publisher hereby disclaims any responsibility for them.

Any people depicted in stock imagery provided by Thinkstock are models, and such images are being used for illustrative purposes only.
Certain stock imagery © Thinkstock.

Cover illustration by Charles Fritz titled, "Captain Lewis Sighting the Yellowstone ~ April 25, 1805." More images and contact information available at charlesfritz.com

Lulu Publishing Services rev. date: 8/1/2017

This book is dedicated to my wife, Dianne, with whom I have shared our wonderful journey.

Contents

Introduction ix
One   *A Most Unusual Corps* 1
Two   *"The Most Friendly and Conciliatory Manner"*. 11
Three   *The Making of a Frontier Hunter* .25
Four   *Pushing Back the Unknown* 43
Five   *Beaver Fever* 55
Six   *Seeking the River's Headwaters*. 65
Seven   *Dying for Business* 75
Eight   *A Kind of Fascination*. 95
Nine   *Returning to Somewhere*. 103
Ten   *No Man's Land* 123
Eleven   *A Cabin on the Boeuf* 137
Twelve   *"A Most Remarkable Man"* 145
Sources Used in Writing This Book 157

Introduction

In the Lakota pantheon, there exists a spirit of the west wind named "Eya." Eya had three brothers each with a distinct personality and unique capabilities. Eya's older brother was Yata, the north wind who by rights owned the birthright from the father Tate. As the four brothers wandered alone across the earth, Eya took the birthright from Yata. Eya took the birthright by an act of courage.

There also existed a fearsome spirit called the "Winged God," who devoured his offspring and destroyed any stranger who ventured into his domain. The Winged God nested in a holy tree, never to be visited by another living creature, divine or otherwise. Eya determined to climb through the tree and nest of the Winged God to encounter the Winged God. While climbing through the nest, Eya encountered a swallow that asked what Eya desired. Eya responded that he was seeking the Winged God. The swallow responded that he would be rewarded for his courage if Eya would give up all pursuit of power and position and become like a ghost among the spirits. Eya agreed to the swallow's terms and became like the swallow and the dog without social position and status. For this sacrifice of self, the Winged God made Eya the first among the four brothers. From henceforth, Eya, the spirit of the west wind, would serve an ungrateful world without reward and recognition.

CHAPTER ONE
A Most Unusual Corps

A warm western wind blew in John Colter's face as he stood atop the high round hill, which now received the body of Charles Floyd. Colter looked towards the frontier, which was like nothing he had ever seen, with its endless bending green grasses and fierce blue sky. Sergeant John Ordway sang a hymn as a prayer for all gathered that bright afternoon.

My life's a shade, my days
Apace to death decline;
My Lord is Life; He'll raise
My dust again, e'en mine.
Sweet truth to me!
I shall arise
And with these eyes
My Saviour see.

No one ever stood next to an occupied open grave and escaped the eternal question of life's end. Now facing unknown peril, each man of the Corps of Discover asked that question silently. George Drouillard looked across the river and thought of old Chief Blackbird buried in those bluffs, but now soaring with his ancestors. Lewis contemplated "dust to dust" and considered the mighty river running below calling him westward. Clark dared not show his tears as he hurt for the loss of a friend and for Charles Floyd's mother and father when they learn of their son's death in a distant land. He took some solace in Ordway's hymn and prayed that the "sweet truth" be true. Young Shannon had not seen as much death as his older Corps members. The great question sank into his psyche and he realized that even he would lie in an open grave. Colter had seen plenty of death in his first 29 years and expected this burial would not be the last he attended. He wondered "what truth" would protect him and bring him home if such a fine man as Sergeant Floyd should die so quickly and needlessly from no injury or apparent malady. (Floyd is said to have died from an appendicitis.)

George Drouillard was an enigma to the men of the Corps. Being half Shawnee, he generated more than a little suspicion and even revulsion when he joined the Corps because some Corps members had buried friends killed by the Shawnee and most members had fought the Shawnee at some time in their recent past. He was a physically impressive man in height and physique, made even more impressive by the eagle and wolf tattoos on his arms and the silver rings in his ears. As days passed, Drouillard became more enigmatic, as he could put a piece of lead through a deer's brain at 150 yards and dress out the carcass in half the time it took most men. He spoke four languages, including English spoken with the French accent inherited from his famous father. Clark was no stranger to the frontier and he could see skills in Drouillard that surpassed the skills of most Corps members. Drouillard's standing with the Corps was not helped by the fact he received a higher wage than the enlisted members of the Corps due to the fact he was hired for his skills and never had enlisted as a soldier. The enlisted men were to receive $5 per month and 320 acres of land while Drouillard was to be paid $25 per month. He performed his duties with a steely confidence and a keenness that could only come from surviving under the most difficult circumstances.

William Clark came from a family of frontier aristocracy. The family still owned land in Virginia proper, but had determined to expand their holdings in the "new Virginia" just south of the Ohio River. These claims would be north of where Daniel Boone chose to claim land in the Bluegrass savannah region. Coming from a family of means and fame did not isolate Clark from frontier hardship, nor did it deny him the experience of depending on others to survive. Living in his famous brothers' shadows motivated him to do great things. Like his brothers, he chose the military to accomplish his personal goals and help provide the necessary protection for the thousands of families venturing across the Appalachian Mountains to claim land for themselves. Frustrated by his lack of promotion and recognition by his military superiors, Clark resigned his commission and returned to his Kentucky home to join the community growing beside the Ohio River. Now at age 33, he accepted an invitation to serve under a younger army "brother" who previously had served under his command.

Meriwether Lewis was in many ways Clark's opposite. Lewis did not have a stable family, having lost his father at an early age. After moving to Georgia with his stepfather and mother, he would escape into the woods where he honed his skills as a hunter with his closest companion, his dog "Ivy." At age 13, Lewis was separated from his beloved woods and Ivy and sent to Virginia for an education where he excelled in all subjects, showed a great curiosity and escaped into the bookshelves of Liberty Hall. Clark had no such inclination nor opportunity for education nor the pursuit of Greek and French ideas. Clark relished an evening campfire with his friends, a good game of cards, sharing a bottle of whisky and the adventure of hunting with friends. Lewis was the personal friend of President Jefferson, while Clark had never visited the new republic's capital. Clark understood the frailties of man, yet still relished their presence. Lewis found many people not to his liking, especially those not embracing the new American ethos founded on virtue. Both men shared personal ambition, a passion for their new republic and a fearless curiosity. Lewis was a driven man. He was driven by his own ambition, his love and loyalty to the president and his unquenchable curiosity. His preparations for the Corps of Discovery had been extensive, including the recruitment of the First Regiment Infantry of the Unites States of American, procurement of three river vessels, studying under several leading minds of the day and purchasing all the necessary items for survival on the frontier plus gifts for the Indians.

George Shannon and John Colter joined Meriwether Lewis at Maysville, Kentucky in September 1803 and they both formally enlisted as privates in the newly formed Corps of Discovery in October. Both of their families were part of a mass western migration when over two hundred thousand citizens of the new Republic walked, rode and floated into Kentucky. Shannon's family floated down the Ohio from Pennsylvania while Colter's family traveled from western Virginia and through the Cumberland Gap. Neither family owned land in the East or much else, but they did possess a hunger for land they could call their own.

The Corps of Discovery wintered in territory possessed by the United States of America across from the Spanish river town of Saint Louis, building Camp Dubois using logs from the surrounding forest. Clark's hut was built last by his order. Several local farmers sold the Corps corn, turnips and beans while the hunters brought ample amounts of fresh meat. Drouillard took great delight in his hunting successes compared to the other hunters and the greatest delight in out-performing Colter and the Fields brothers. Drouillard was beaten in a shooting contest by Reubin Fields, which did hurt his pride, but shooting contests were not something he had experienced before.

Shooting contests, various games, hunting, carpentry, blacksmithing and army drilling kept the men busy through the winter. To keep them happy, the officers provided whiskey to each man every day. In addition to their daily allotment, Corps members were rewarded for good work with a double ration of whiskey. The keelboat was loaded with whiskey when it landed near Camp Dubois and by the end of the Corps' journey more than twenty-five hundred bottles of the frontier's "finest" whiskey would be consumed by the Corps members. Being subject to the officers' ration did not deter the men from finding a local supply of whiskey from taverns near Camp Debois. After several weeks of extended "hunting" forays, Lewis realized that these trips were nothing but a "pretext for visiting a neighboring whiskey shop." With this discovery, Lewis confined several men to quarters for ten days, including John Colter.

On New Year's Eve day while Lewis was absent from the camp, Colter and several Corps members walked into Rumsey's tavern for a drinking binge. Colter's group was a diverse collection of frontier men, Easterners, professional soldiers, Kentucky militia, younger and older Corps members. What they had in common was the restless quest for a whiskey escape from the discipline of the officers and the drudgery of Camp Dubois.

Colter was a quiet man who preferred the corner of the room, until he drank whiskey. Colter was quite fond of the frontier elixir. Having been raised in BlueGrass country, he was well acquainted with Kentucky whisky. As his trapping and hunting business developed, he found even better whiskey on the Ohio River where he sold his furs and skins. Rumsey was well acquainted with Colter as he had made several "hunting" trips to his establishment. It was a cold New Year's Eve, so Rumsey had the fire well stoked and the small box of a room was warm enough for the fur coats to come off.

After three generous gills, Colter's whisky personality emerged and things started to get testy. After hearing several stories of heroism from the professional soldiers in the group, Colter railed at their ignorance of frontier survival and their dismissal of Indian bravery. Truth be known, the soldiers in the group had never faced an Indian charge in battle nor seen the deadly accuracy of an arrow flying so fast it was barely visible. Colter laid it on, recounting how the Kentuckians had won all the shooting contests and the soldiers were recruited to push the keelboat up the river and nothing else. Hugh Hall, being a soldier from Pennsylvania, had heard enough and told Colter to shut his "ignorant backwoods mouth" or he would shut it for him. Luckily for all present, Colter's knife, tomahawk and gun were at Camp Dubois, but unfortunately for Hall, Colter had his deadly quick fist, which found Hall's jaw, dropping him on Rumsey's floor. While this was not a sobering event, it did bring the evening to an end as Hall was picked up and taken back to the camp and Colter bought one more drink before grabbing his fur coat and meandering among the trees, watching a fox creep across his path and "hearing" an owl watching him from its perch.

When Colter reached Camp Dubois, he saw the outline of a solitary figure standing at the Camp entrance with arms folded. As Colter approached, he realized that it was Sergeant Ordway who would command Colter's squad. Colter was not a "military man" and Ordway was the epitome of one. To make matters worse, Colter's slow walk back to the Camp gave Hall's helpers a chance to relate the events and words involving Colter. Hall and Ordway had served together on the frontier and both were "Easterners." Colter knew Ordway could not be happy, but he had never seen Ordway happy in any circumstance, so nothing would surprise him. Ordway's stance and stillness confirmed Colter's thought that he was being harshly judged by this son of the Puritans and who thought Colter to be an uneducated, godless, drunk. As Colter trudged into the camp, Ordway said not one word.

Word reached Camp Dubois that the territory known as "Louisiana" was being purchased from the French. This development brought great excitement to the men of the Corps as their mission acquired more importance in service to their country. The official transfer of territory was to occur in Saint Louis and authorities there invited both Lewis and Clark to attend the ceremonies and the formal balls celebrating the purchase of Louisiana. These events would entail many days absent from Camp Dubois, so Lewis chose Ordway to take command of the camp in the officers' absence. In doing so, he wrote specific directions for camp projects and activities to be directed by Ordway and wrote a specific order that anyone leaving the camp must have Ordway's permission with the exception of the hunters, and even the hunters must serve guard duty. Only those engaged in carpentry and blacksmithing would be relieved of the dreaded guard duty.

The third day after Lewis and Clark departed, several hunters left the camp to fulfill their duties. Robert Frazer was a longtime acquaintance of Colter having moved from the same Virginia county to the Kentucky Bluegrass. Frazer was a decent hunter, but Colter was the best tracker in the outfit and could shoot as well as Frazer. The recent snow made tracking deer particularly easy and by midday they had killed and dressed four deer. With a good day's work already completed, Colter suggested they "warm up" at Rumsey's and Frazer agreed.

Meanwhile, Reubin Fields was having equally good fortune with his hunting and started bringing his dressed deer into the camp in early afternoon. Having lugged three deer some distance to the camp, he was well worn and drenched with sweat. As he delivered his last deer to the mess, Sergeant Ordway commanded him to stand guard duty for the next four hours. Fields, like most of the Kentucky hunters, did not think much of military order and especially the type of order coming from Ordway. Fields flatly refused the order and started to leave the mess. As Ordway's voice rose threatening a court martial, another Kentuckian, John Shields, joined the shouting match protesting that Ordway was being unreasonable by asking the worn-out Fields to stand guard duty and suggested one of the "lazy" soldiers who had been making sugar take the next guard duty. Shields was one of the oldest members of the Corps and the Kentuckians looked up to him as a skillful carpenter, blacksmith, gunsmith and hunter. Shields embraced this role and proceeded to get between Ordway and Fields, scolding Ordway and his fellow soldiers for not "carrying their weight" while enjoying the meat so generously provided by the Kentucky hunters. By now several other members of the Corps had emerged to witness this confrontation. As tempers were boiling over, Sergeant Floyd joined the group and standing next to Ordway suggested that Fields take a turn on guard duty later that evening. Fields agreed and stomped off with Shields while Ordway grumbled that Floyd was too easy on the men.

As the winter sun was setting over the Mississippi, two very drunk hunters asked the guard on duty, who happened to be Fields, for permission to enter the camp. Fields gave his permission and warned Frazer and Colter to go straight to their hut and avoid Ordway at all costs. As they crossed the parade grounds headed to their hut they made several loud announcements about their hunting success and denounced the duty of sugar making as woman's work. These "announcements" were heard by many, including Ordway who followed the two drunks into their hut. Ordway told Frazer and Colter that he was putting them on report and they would likely face a court martial trial upon the return of Lewis and Clark. Colter dared him to take such drastic action and dismissed the likelihood of any consequences because the soldiers in camp would likely starve without him feeding them. This exchange confirmed Ordway's impression that the Corps was doomed to insubordination and chaos unless he instilled more discipline. While he could not control these unruly Kentuckians, he could control what they could eat and drink and where they could go, so he confined them to their hut until the Officers returned and denied them their daily gill of whisky. Colter had heard enough and picked up his rifle and started priming it when Ordway charged him, took the gun and pushed him to the floor as Frazer watched in disbelief.

Lewis returned from Saint Louis before Clark and received a full report from Ordway. Lewis was "mortified and disappointed at the disorderly conduct" of the men, which fed growing concerns about the success of the Corps and the challenge of keeping military discipline in this collection of men. After reviewing Ordway's report and conferring with Sergeant Floyd, Lewis decided to hold a trial of Shields, Colter and Frazer and confer a lighter punishment on Fields. A military court martial trial could result in expulsion from the unit or corporal punishment if not expulsion. The months spent at Camp Dubois were a final opportunity for Lewis and Clark to evaluate the assembled men. Not all men would be selected for the exploration all the way to the Pacific. Some men would be chosen to return to Saint Louis from the first winter quarters and others would be rejected for any duty.

Upon Clark's return from Saint Louis, the officers appointed a sergeant as judge, a jury of four and a judge advocate. The trial began with the reading of the charges written by Lewis. When informed of the insubordination, Clark was concerned about the discipline needed for the Corps to survive, but equally concerned with the importance of each man to the success of the unit. He was quite familiar with the enmity between frontier militia and the professional military, having seen this during the Ohio campaigns against the Shawnee, and he doubted there was a skilled Kentucky hunter who would not chafe at military discipline. Clark convinced Lewis to press lesser charges in an effort to avoid splitting the Corps or losing some of the most skilled frontiersmen in the unit. Colter greatly regretted his actions, which now endangered his future with the Corps. His drinking had once again been excessive and destructive. He was not an introspective person, but on this occasion, he wondered about his desire for liquor in excess and his regretful behavior. He could find no explanation or justification for this with the possible exception of just being bored.

The three were found guilty and required to stand before the Corps on the parade grounds and confess, offer an apology and swear to follow orders from all superiors in the future. This was done as required with Colter and Shields offering such heartfelt statements that when Clark posted the list of men selected to the permanent Corps detachment, both men's names were on the list. Frazer was demoted to the detachment returning from the first winter quarters. The leniency shown Colter and Shields and their inclusion in the permanent detachment clearly reflected their unique skills and importance to the Corps. Additionally, their heartfelt statements on the parade grounds revealed a profound desire to be part of something as challenging and important as the Corps of Discovery.

As the Corps descended the steep bluff where Sergeant Floyd now lay, the hired French river men were preparing the Corps' three boats for the next move up the river. The Corps pushed a little distance to the mouth of a small river that Clark named Floyd to honor his friend "who had at all times given proof of his sincerity and good will to serve his country." There they would spend the night in preparation for their push into the land of the Sioux and the open Plains.

CHAPTER TWO
"The Most Friendly and Conciliatory Manner"

Shields and Fields returned to the river not having found Shannon. Shannon and Drouillard had been sent to find the four horses that had been left grazing on the grasslands above the Missouri's high bank. Drouillard worked best alone and he certainly did not need the company of Shannon, so he told young Shannon to head north in search for the horses and he would head east. This was a logical move, but also a reflection of Drouillard's contempt for Shannon who was as "green" as Drouillard was hardened by experience. Now Shannon was lost hurrying to find the horses to prove his place in the Corps and gain the confidence of his more experienced comrades. As the youngest member of the Corps and one of Lewis's choices, there was great skepticism about this George Shannon. What did Lewis see in this young man? He did not have the frontier skills of Colter who also joined the Corps at Maysville. Clark acknowledged the fact that Shannon was not a "first rate hunter." Now Clark faced losing a second Corps member early in their journey. Lewis said nothing either from embarrassment or concern as he and Clark discussed the disappearance of Shannon and how to retrieve him to safety. Clark begrudgingly told Lewis that they should dispatch one of the skilled Corps trackers to bring young Shannon back and his choice was John Colter.

With no horses now available, Colter returned to the river bank where Shannon and Drouillard had set out to find the horses two days ago. The footprints were easy to pick up and he could see where Drouillard and Shannon split in their search. Drouillard was a big man, so it was easy to identify Shannon's footprints heading north in search of the horses. It was apparent that Shannon was moving at a fast pace. Shannon's footprints were not the only footprints left along the Missouri. Heading north toward the river, Colter crossed two different sets of tracks that could be nothing other than Sioux Indians heading back to their villages on the other side of the Missouri. Colter recollected that several days prior, the Corps had encountered Frenchman Pierre Dorion, who was married to a Sioux woman and was very friendly toward the Yankton Sioux. Colter hoped that Dorion's description of the "friendly" Yankton Sioux would hold true if he encountered them along the Missouri.

Late in the day, Shannon's tracks could be seen going up the side of the riverbank and into the grasses of the flowing plain. The Missouri River was now running west to east and the Plains were much flatter, allowing for a more distant surveillance. Even with this greater visibility, Shannon and the horses were nowhere to be seen. The grass was tall and thick, giving the horses a feast and a reward for their wandering. Colter now realized that this assignment was not going to be accomplished quickly and started looking for a place to spend the night. Wearing just his buckskins and no fur would not be a problem as the weather was still warm, and sleeping in the grass would provide a comfortable "bed" for the night.

As some cranes on the river squawked at the rising sun, Colter grabbed his specially designed short rifle and started hunting for breakfast. Lewis had issued one of his specially designed rifles to him, which he greatly appreciated, given its shorter 34-inch length and lighter weight. He had experience tracking in grass in the Kentucky savannah and soon found a trail going down to the river. Colter knew that the first key in the hunt is seeing the prey before it sees or smells you, which required stalking in dips and folds rather than on ridges or hilltops and staying upwind. Moving away from the river in one of those prairie dips he spotted his prey some two hundred yards to the south and with a westerly breeze moving the grasses there was no way his scent would be detected by the group of grazing buffalo. With limited cover to hide his presence, he found some tall bluestem in which to quietly stalk closer to the buffalo enjoying the prairie grass "breakfast." Little did the buffalo know, one of their group was about to be Colter's breakfast. It was an easy choice as a large bull was the closest in the group and he would provide Colter and the Corps a fine meal. While the short rifle was accurate and generated a high speed projectile, it afforded only one shot as the muzzle reloading could take over a minute. This would not be a problem as Colter aligned the gun's sights and gently squeezed the trigger and watched the bull's knees buckle and drop as the remaining buffalo abandoned him. There would be no tracking down a wounded animal as Colter had put his lead through the animal's head. Removing the buffalo's insides required little time, but quartering the carcass, moving the quarters to the river and cutting strips would take most of the day. This two-thousand-pound bull would provide five hundred and fifty pounds of raw meat and after being dried, two hundred seventy-five pounds of protein for the Corps. Colter could have selected the loin cuts and enjoyed his breakfast quickly, but he understood his priority was to be keep the Corps supplied with meat. Shannon was a lower priority and Colter would rather hunt game than hunt Shannon. Colter carried the meat to the river and built a scaffold along the river and put the strips of buffalo meat in the sun to dry, high enough so the prairie animals could not take his prey. If the Indians discovered the scaffold, he was out of luck.

On the third day of tracking Shannon, Colter noted that Shannon had overtaken the horses and had started riding the horses west along the Missouri. It was apparent to Colter that Shannon was moving west to overtake the Corps when in fact the Corps was well behind him. The chase up the river proved to Colter why Shannon should have stayed in Maysville. A quick calculation should have convinced him that the fast-moving Missouri kept the Corp moving at a slow enough pace that he should have overtaken them by now. Shannon was now riding horses and moving at a pace that proved too fast for Colter, so after six days of searching, Colter concluded that "the fool was on his own" and gave up the chase and returned to the Corps. Clark also determined that Shannon was now on his own and no further efforts would be made to find him. When informed of Clark's decision, Lewis was incensed and sulked in the keelboat cabin for the remainder of the day and night. During the night, a ferocious storm blew in from the west and Lewis pondered how young Shannon might endure such wind and rain without protection and provisions.

During his return to the Corps, Colter killed an elk, three deer, one wolf, five turkeys, one beaver and one goose. Felling the goose in flight with the somewhat accurate short rifle and its hefty .54 caliber projectile was something few of the Corps could do. Colter took great satisfaction in his hunting successes as the Corps found two Colter scaffolds loaded with dried meat as it moved up the river.

The Yankton Sioux reception was a huge success! President Jefferson directed Lewis to engage the native populations "in the most friendly & conciliatory manner which their own conduct will admit." Jefferson and Lewis knew that the French and English had traded with these communities for decades and the Americans were the newcomers. Jefferson also knew about the strength and importance of the Sioux Indians and in his Lewis orders stated "we wish more particularly to make a favorable impression, because of their power." Now that Louisiana belonged to the fledging republic, the native populations must understand this and direct their commerce and fealty to the United States. Lewis developed a speech to convey this to each tribe the Corps encountered and it would be translated by Drouillard or a local recruit. In this case, Dorion would serve nicely as he had lived with the Yankton for twenty years as a French trader and spoke the Siouan languages of both the Yankton Dakota and the Brule Lakota. Clark knew of the old Frenchman from his brother, George Rogers Clark, who had been in contact with him during the war to free America from Britain.

When a young Yankton boy swam up to the keelboat and informed Lewis of a nearby Yankton encampment, an excited Lewis directed Dorion and Sergeant Nathaniel Pryor to travel to the encampment and invite their leaders to join them for a council on a nearby bluff. Upon their arrival at the encampment, Pryor was welcomed as an honored guest and the leaders, Weuche, White Crane and Half Man quickly accepted the invitation to council.

As the Corps had done previously with the Otoes and Missouris, the officers and army enlisted men donned their dress uniforms and formed ranks in a formal gesture of respect to their hosts. With equal pomp, the chiefs followed singers and drummers to the council site. The council began with the necessary introductions followed by a speech by Lewis. Lewis had encountered Indians in Georgia and in Ohio while serving in the army, but he had never conducted warfare, commerce or friendship with any Indian populations. His approach to the Yankton was stiff and paternalistic. The three chiefs gathered under an awning near the boat and under the American flag that cracked in the northwest wind sweeping the bluff.

> "Children
> . – It gives us much pleasure to have met you here this day in council. We salute you as the children of your Great Father the great Chief of the Seventeen Great Nations of America. We see around us a number of the Old and experienced, the wise men and Warriors of the Soues nation.
> Children
> . – It will please your Great Father when he is informed of the readiness with which you have assembled yourselves to hear good councils which he has commanded us to give you.
> Children
> . – Now open your ears that you may hear his words, and dispose your minds to understand them. Reflect on the time past, and that to come; do not deceive yourselves, nor suffer others to deceive you, but like men and warriors devoted to the real interest of their nation; seek those truths, which can alone perpetuate its happiness
> ---
> Children
> . – Commissioned and sent by the Great Chief of the Seventeen Great Nations of America, we have come to inform you, as we go also to inform all the nations of red men who inhabit the borders of the Missouri, that a great Council was lately held between this great Chief of the Seventeen Great Nations of America, and your Old fathers the French and Spaniards. In this council it was agreed that all the white men on the waters of the Missouri and Mississippi, should obey the commands

of the Great Chief of America, who has adopted them as his children, and they now form one Common family with us. Your old traders are of this description; they are no longer the subjects of France or Spain, but have become the citizens of the Seventeen Great Nations of America, and are bound to obey the commands of their great chief the President, who is now your only great father.

Children

. – This Council being concluded between your old Fathers the French and Spaniards, and your great father the great Chief of the Seventeen Great Nations of America, your Old fathers the French and Spaniards in Compliance with their engagements made in that council, have withdrawn all their troops from all their Military Ports on the Waters of the Missouri and Mississippi, and have surrendered to our great chief all their fortifications and Land in this Country, together with the mouths of all the Rivers through which the traders bring goods to the red men on the troubled waters."

Following the Lewis speech, the chiefs speaking through Dorion expressed their desire for peace and trade. At the conclusion of the ceremony and speech, the Corps fired their guns, including the air gun brought by Lewis, which made a frightening thunder-like boom. The chiefs were given flags and clothing, which they graciously received, and shook hands with the officers. All agreed to meet the following morning to discuss the issues and needs of both parties.

With less formality the next morning, the officers joined the chiefs for a parley. Weuche took the lead and in a very urgent and firm tone asked the officers for guns. Like most of the Plains Indians, the Yankton had been pushed west by European and Indian competition for farmland and hunting grounds. The Sioux had crossed into the Missouri River area just thirty years prior to the Corps' arrival. The Yankton, like the other Sioux, had fallen into a geographic void left by tribes depleted by devastating diseases brought by white men. Their good fortune was to inhabit a land teaming with buffalo and other game, but their bad fortune was the number of other tribes that preceded the Sioux into the Plains and were seeking the same buffalo with the modern technologies of pony and gun. Any tribe that cultivated relationships with the French or British first gained access to guns and ammunition. The Yankton had no such relationship with the French and British, so the Americans were to be the answer to their most pressing need for survival.

Lewis had no intention of satisfying the Yankton's request for guns. The keelboat was loaded with gifts to gain favor with each tribe they met, but arming any one tribe was not in the plan. He was aware of the contentious relationship between tribes and Jefferson wanted the Corps to be a mission of peace and harmony among Indians of the Louisiana Purchase. What Jefferson and Lewis did not understand was the web of alliances and shifting balance of power among the Plains Indians. Any foreign power could easily upset the alliances and relationships among the tribes. Lewis sought a peaceful frontier that would allow American commerce to flourish. While Jefferson was seeking a vast amount of scientific information from the Corps, there can be no doubt that commerce was a high priority. Finding a route to the Pacific was primarily driven by a desire to secure commerce in the Northwest where the British were already making inroads. In his letter to Lewis, he stated, "The commerce which may be carried on with the people inhabiting the line you will pursue, renders a knowledge of those people important." Congress legislated the relationship between whites and the native population with several legislative efforts including the Nonintercourse Act giving the federal government control over all commerce with the native populations and excluding state claims that were being made at the time. This act gave substance to the Constitution's clause giving Congress all power to regulate commerce with the Indian tribes. The act established the federal government as the sole entity permitted to regulate trade with the native populations and established "factories," which were officially licensed trading posts where the native populations could sell their merchandise.

Given the weak geopolitical position of the Yankton, they would accept the new relationship with the Great Father in Washington. As the council was concluding, Chief Half Man wished the Corps well as they travelled up the river, but offered a warning: "those nations above will not open their ears, and you cannot I fear open them."

While Lewis and the Yankton chiefs were joining in council, Colter was on the prairie looking for Shannon. After the Yankton council and Colter's return, the Corps began moving up the river. On September 11, 1804, a member of the Corps spotted a lone horse and human figure on the riverbank. Shannon was nearly starved, having not eaten anything but grapes and one rabbit over the previous twelve days of his separation from the Corps. What started as an opportunity to prove his worth now exposed Shannon as the young, inexperienced Corps member that he truly was. His only success was the one horse he found and returned to the Corps.

Colter resumed his efforts to provision the Corps with meat from his hunting sojourns ahead of the Corps. There was much talk in the Corps about the expected encounter with the troublesome Teton Sioux mentioned by Half Man. As Colter rode the Corps' horse up the river he spotted several elk on a large island in the wide Missouri where it began a big turn to the north. With the wind behind him, he turned his horse and found a trail over the river embankment and onto the prairie where he could ride above and around the island and be upwind from the elk. Colter knew that the men of the Corps especially enjoyed fresh elk meat, so this was an opportunity to provide them with the pleasure of elk steaks. Guiding his horse down the embankment into the river and on to the island, he used the cottonwood trees to provide cover for his approach to the grazing elk. After covering half the length of the island, Colter dismounted and tied his horse to a cottonwood then took his short rifle and ammunition pouch in search of the elk grazing beyond the cottonwoods. Moving into the wind and behind the trees, he could now see the elk some 150 yards down the island. Given the ideal conditions, he felt no need to get closer and risk discovery by the herd, so he removed the sling and rifle from his shoulder then primed his flintlock, having already pushed his powder and projectile down the rifle barrel. He had learned that preparing the barrel was best done after spotting his prey, but not while stalking his prey. Aligning his sights on his long barrel he pulled the trigger and watched one elk drop in a heap. Surprisingly, the other elk did not immediately scatter with the crack of his rifle, so he began the process of reloading and once again aiming and dropping a second elk. The Corps would be most pleased with his double kill.

With two elk down and ready to be dressed, Colter returned to the Cottonwood where he had tied the Corps' horse. Upon locating the tree, the horse was nowhere to be seen. Looking for any tracks that might guide his pursuit of the horse, Colter could plainly see the horse tracks and the moccasin tracks of Indians who must have stolen the horse. Stealing a horse was considered one of the highest accomplishments of a Plains Indian. Given their nomadic existence, the horse was the most valuable asset of a family and village, so stealing a horse brought great honor and respect to the warrior who accomplished the feat. It was said that a skillful warrior could "crawl into a bivouac where a dozen men were sleeping, each with his horse tied to this wrist by a lariat, cut a rope within six feet of the sleeper's person, and get off with the horse without waking a soul." Colter could see the Corps coming up the river and ran down to the end of the island to inform the officers of his kill and the loss of his horse. Clark ordered a pirogue to retrieve the two elk, dress them and bring the fresh meat aboard the keelboat. As this was occurring, five Indians on the river's bank called and asked to come aboard the keelboat. One of the Frenchman answered in the Nemaha language, which they did not understand. Dorion was no longer with the Corps and communications were quickly a problem during this first encounter with the mighty Teton Sioux. After more discussion, the five Teton understood that any further interaction with the Corps was conditional on the return of the stolen horse. With this concern understood, the officers asked for a council with the Teton chiefs in the morning.

When Colter pulled his fur blanket over him that night, he thought of how he had been watched by the Teton as they waited for their opportunity to steal his horse. How close had they been? Next time it could be his scalp they took. He had had no inkling that he was the hunted. He was the hunter, not the hunted. In a forest maybe, but how was it the Teton had kept themselves hidden and stolen his horse on the island? Perhaps it was his focus on the elk. How easy it was to be blind to threats so near. Just as the elk were overly engaged with the succulent grass, Colter put himself in peril by ignoring his surroundings and the potential threats to him. A good hunter must be part of his surroundings with an eye for the twitch of an ear and an ear for the snap of a twig. His last thought before sleep overcame him was that a Teton had never been part of his surroundings before.

Survival drew a dividing line between the Europeans crowding into the eastern coast of the United States and the frontiersmen and Indians of the Plains. The Europeans saw survival relative to their personal accomplishments and status in the social and economic community at large. To survive in the European world depended on individual initiative and self-improvement. Control over one's destiny and "survival" depended on individual initiative. Living on the frontier was a dicey role dependent on weather, community strength and the actions of unfriendly communities nearby. One failed crop or one failed hunting season meant disaster. One disease or community disagreement could destroy a community. One hostile neighboring community, whether they be English, Shawnee or Cree, that found new allies or new weapons would spell the end for their neighbors. No community understood this better than the Teton Sioux Indians who had barely survived their past and now had a resolve to survive in the future.

The Sioux people had been a sedentary community in the Great Lakes region living among the hardwood forests where game was plentiful and rain and the growing season were sufficient to grow maize. The balance of the indigenous communities in the area was upset when Europeans brought iron goods and muskets into the region. The Hudson Bay Company aligned itself with the Iron Confederacy composed of Cree, Ojibwa(Chippewa) and Assiniboine communities. These communities were feeling some pressure from eastern tribes as they pushed west to find new ground not claimed by Europeans. The Iron Confederacy served the newly arrived Hudson Bay Company very well as the middlemen of the growing trade of European iron goods for Indian furs and skins. Unlike the French, the British had no desire to inhabit and mix with the indigenous communities, so having a large community to act as a middleman to the multitude of tribes in the fur-rich frontier was a sound strategy. One community not trading with the Iron Confederacy was the Sioux community, which had a long enmity and contempt toward both the Ojibwa and Assiniboine communities. As the Iron Confederacy prospered, its numbers grew and they used their superior weaponry to push the Sioux out of the Great Lakes region into the unfamiliar savannah, where few trees existed, the cropping was limited and winters were horrendous.

The Sioux community started to fragment during this migration. The Plains could not support large populations in one location due to the limited water, game and growing conditions, so individual bands of Sioux formed. The saving resource for the Teton band and the Yankton was the buffalo. During the buffalo hunt the bands would cooperate to maximize the success of the hunt. The buffalo hunt required each band to be very mobile, so the Sioux culture became nomadic, thanks to horses they could steal or gain through trading with other Indians. In a relatively short period of time the Sioux became the most accomplished horsemen on the Plains as it was a critical part of their survival.

The Sioux added another element to their survival plan and that was controlling the trade on the Missouri River. If the Sioux could keep the British, French, Spanish and now the Americans from trading with upriver communities, they could become middlemen like the Iron Confederacy. They would use their stranglehold on the river to require the Europeans and Americans to trade with them on terms favorable to them and then trade the European goods for furs, skins and maize supplied by the upriver communities. An important element of this trade would involve trading with the upriver Arikara communities that had mastered maize production in their sedentary villages.

The council with the Teton began as the other had begun with the Lewis speech, a military parade, the giving of gifts, the demonstration of weaponry and the demand for the return of the stolen horse. The Teton chiefs were not impressed. To add to the complexities of the geopolitical and economic realities and the lack of an interpreter, the leadership of the Teton was in turmoil. Leadership among most of the Plains Indians was earned through deeds and wisdom. Any politicking or attempts to claim the chief position were signs of weakness. The two contenders were Black Buffalo and Tortohongar, known to the white traders as "The Partisan." Black Buffalo led the larger village on the banks of the Missouri River while The Partisan led the smaller village up the Bad River, which fed into the Missouri. Lewis made a big mistake by taking Black Buffalo to be the Number One chief and lavishing him with gifts not given to The Partisan. After realizing that they were making no progress, Lewis and Clark invited the chiefs on to the keelboat for further discussions using Drouillard's sign language. The hospitality included whiskey which was the second big Lewis mistake and made any further discussion impossible. Clark asked Colter, Drouillard and the Fields brothers to join him in returning the chiefs to the riverbank. As the small boat approached the bank, several warriors grabbed the bow line and held on to it. As The Partisan disembarked, he pushed Clark causing him to draw his sword and Colter and the others to raise their rifles. Colter knew the odds were impossible with their single shot rifles, but he would make sure The Partisan would not live to brag about stopping the Corps of Discovery. Black Buffalo quickly came between the two protagonists and ordered the warriors to drop the bowline. Black Buffalo quickly convened a huddle with the elders and The Partisan, resulting in a cooler situation. Clark offered to shake hands with the assembly, but none would accept his gesture. He agreed to another council in the morning and Black Buffalo's request to spend the night on the keelboat.

    The next day the Teton tried another approach and offered an invitation to feast followed by entertainment in the village. As they passed through the village, Colter was impressed with the ornate teepees, well dressed women and children and the overall health of the entire village. There were many horses in the village, partly due to the recent raid on an Omaha village, which had resulted in many horses being taken, as well as hostages. After their night of enjoyment, the next day brought on more clumsy discussions and more intransigence on the part of the Teton. The Partisan asked to spend the night on the keelboat in an effort not to be outdone by Black Buffalo. As the small boat approached the keelboat at dusk, it cut the anchor rope causing orders to be yelled and great commotion as the Americans jumped to action to gain control of the keelboat. All this commotion alerted the villagers who thought the

Omaha were attacking. Within minutes the riverbank was lined with two hundred warriors; when Black Buffalo realized there was no threat and he asked the warriors to stand down. Colter spent another sleepless night with his rifle loaded with powder.

The next morning Lewis and Clark decided it was time to move up the river. They planned to return The Partisan to the riverbank in a small boat with Lewis and Clark remaining on the keelboat. Sergeant Ordway and the same four men who accompanied Clark, including Colter, would accompany The Partisan as the crew prepared to depart. As this was being executed, The Partisan noted the preparations and upon disembarking ordered his warriors to grab the anchor line. As the men returned to the keelboat, the four men jumped into the water near the boat and grabbed the anchor line as it rose into the boat causing it to slip through the warriors' hands. Clark aimed the swivel gun at the Teton on the riverbank, which Black Buffalo noted with grave concern. Not wanting to endanger his village, he yelled to Lewis to swing a crate of tobacco toward the warriors, which he did giving the flotilla the time to move up the river without the approval of the Teton. A soaking John Colter stood on the keelboat deck watching the Teton disappear downstream thinking how different they were from the previous river communities encountered and how determined they were to control events and ultimately their future. The keelboat sailed north toward the villages of the Arikara communities.

CHAPTER THREE
The Making of a Frontier Hunter

The Colters were Virginians from the Shenandoah region, not the tidewater. Like most folks living in Augusta County, the Colters were farmers, not aristocrats. Virginia as a colony and then a state claimed large areas of land west of the Appalachian Mountains. The British attempted to keep the Virginians from settling in these western areas and outlawed any such attempt. This effort was only partially successful and with the conclusion of the Revolutionary War, the gates were open for westward movement and settlement.

John Colter's father was not the eldest son and as such would not inherit land. He learned of the vast tracts of Kentucky land that were being settled by Virginians from the Shenandoah Valley and how productive this virgin land was for farming. So when John was still a boy, the Colters moved down the Wilderness Road and through the Cumberland Pass into the quickly populating Bluegrass region of central Kentucky. The Bluegrass savannah of central Kentucky was a mixture of nutrient-rich grasses and occasional deciduous trees that provided a favorable mixture of open farmland and wood for buildings and fuel. Anyone moving into the area had to know how to handle an ax and fire weapons or they would not be on the frontier for long. While neighborliness and community spirit were strong, there were limits. Felling trees and busting sod was hard work. Young John Colter detested both and chafed under his father's work assignments in starting a farm, but he did enjoy and learn a lifelong skill from his father. One of the family's few valuable possessions was their 42-inch-long Kentucky rifle and Colter's father taught his son the fine art and science of loading, aiming and maintaining this piece of technology. Another skill learned early by John was the ability to identify a footprint or trace of any creature known to the area and to track the creature through fields, forest and streams. This skill served him well in hunting and trapping animals.

By the time John was 16, he had a reputation for his skills in hunting and trapping. Abandoning his father's desire for John to be a farmer, John endeavored to make a living hunting and trapping. This choice of hunting and trapping was not popular with his family and caused bad feelings. The farmer was considered to be more virtuous and the backbone of republicanism. The hunter could not sustain his position in the community nor the economy as he relied on a depletable resource and was prone to absences from family and community. While hunting down animals that threatened the farm and community was acceptable and even hunting for a source of protein was acceptable, the frontier communities were to be built around planted crops and animal husbandry. The arrival of Europeans to the Eastern Seaboard of North American had already greatly depleted the wildlife necessary for supporting the growing demand for protein, skins and furs, so animal husbandry developed east of the Appalachians while hunting and trapping wild animals prospered west of the Appalachian Mountains.

Colter did not much like the farmers his age who chose to clear their land, get married and start having children. To him, this was slavery to the family and the tyranny of nature. If a man could make a living hunting and trapping wherever he pleased, he could be free of the bonds of nature, family and community. Getting up early in the morning and venturing into the woodland alive with the stirrings of its creatures gave each day an optimism of its own. Searching for fresh tracks or checking traps was freedom. The community wondered about John's hunting and why he was not spending time in his father's field. This proved to be somewhat of an embarrassment to the Colter family having a man-son still living at home, but the Colter family always had meat on the table and fat aplenty for soaps, candles and foods. John enjoyed his successful hunts and when he had more than enough for the family he would share his plenty with neighbors who were suffering for lack of meat and fat. The need for protein and skins in central Kentucky provided Colter an opportunity to supply family and community, but there was no real cash market for skins and furs. The best and closest market for furs was sixty-four miles north on the Ohio River at Maysville, which fed the various French trading posts and ultimately New Orleans with products destined for Europe. As a result, John was known to both the Maysville community and the community of his family in central Kentucky.

One family that respected John and lived nearby was the Davis family. They liked John's easy manner and John liked them because they respected him and his hunting skills. They were the first to get the surplus of his hunting efforts. Nathan Davis was older than John, but younger than John's father. He was less judgmental of young John's hunting pursuits and often complimented him on his success. The mutual respect was shared with Nathan's wife, Sarah, who was quick to invite John to dinner with the six children when preparing the venison brought to their home by John. The children reminded him of the bondage he wanted to avoid, but the family had a joy and firmness he appreciated. It was more than just shelter and food, there was a warmth and strength in the family as grace was offered and food was respectfully passed.

While the Davis family made him yearn for something he did not have, another neighbor, Forrest Hancock, shared the life chosen by John. He was single, embraced the hunting and trapping life and was pushed to the periphery of the community. John and Forrest would often meet early in the morning for their hunting and trapping sojourns then finish the day in O'Shea's tavern. They were married to the forest and the hunt and took great pride in their skill and knowledge they developed compared to the men who worked the fields. Their interest in women was tempered by the demographic fact that men far outnumbered women on the frontier. The birth of many children on the frontier resulted in the death of many mothers. Fathers without a wife and with young children would resolve their situation either by quickly remarrying or by sending children away to be raised. In addition, the frontier call appealed to more men than women, so many younger men would venture into Kentucky to stake claims, clear trees and build homes in preparation for a wife or family living in Virginia. An available twenty-year-old female was as rare as an albino doe.

Young John's easy relationships with Forrest and the Davis family suddenly collided when Nathan Davis injured himself chopping wood.

On an icy February morning, Nathan slipped causing him to bury his ax in his foot. John Colter did everything he could to help the struggling Davis family. Nathan's pain and the inconvenience of the injury grew more serious with a creeping green moving up his leg, which took his life. The community hurt from Nathan's death and surrounded Sarah with support. Wood was plentiful for warmth, repairs of the home were made, material for the children's clothes was delivered and John made sure that food was on the table. The nagging question regarding the Davis family was spring planting and the fall harvest. Who would fill this most pressing void left by Nathan Davis? John Colter felt this void. He yearned for the warmth and strength of family that Nathan and Sarah created, but he rebelled at the idea of felling trees, plowing ground and harvesting grain for the Davis family. He could see the invitation in Sarah's eyes, which was partly desire, but mostly desperation. He was needed, how could he turn his back on Sarah and the children? He was not a planter nor a harvester and had never said an audible prayer in his life.

On one of John's food deliveries to the Davis home, Sarah asked John to join the family for dinner. John reluctantly accepted the invitation, feeling the pressure to accept as a friend and to lend some hope to the family's uncertain future. While the small community around the Davis family was very supportive, there was a growing feeling of desperation that the loss of one provider put a burden on the entire community. Would the entire community have to support the Davis family, meaning all would have to get by with less? There was even some talk of sending them back to Virginia to her family there.

John brought a nice elk quarter to the Davis house and some small wood figures he had carved for the smaller children. He remembered having similar figures that he enjoyed as a small boy as he pretended the figures were frontier hunters fearlessly hunting dangerous bears and Indians. As the door opened, he saw the face of six-year-old Joshua who was a favorite of his. Joshua adored John and he was watching for John's arrival. If John could have Sarah and Joshua to start his family all would be fine, but six children and a farm to manage were too much. Sarah greeted John with her usual smile and polite manner, which John found attractive and warm. Sarah was eight years older than John and she knew the frontier had taken its toll on her appearance, but this night in the firelight she was not a widow but a woman ready to move on with her life. There was no desperation in her, but warm hospitality and an inviting manner.

The two oldest children dished up the potatoes and beans that would accompany the elk meat that John had provided. As the family sat down for dinner, John noticed the empty chair at the head of the table and respectfully sat next to Joshua on the side bench. Isaac, the oldest boy, offered a grace that included thanks for John's presence and generosity. John had never thought of himself as an instrument of God, but was touched by the graciousness of the eldest son and John thought of what a fine father Nathan had been. John enjoyed the meal, but found the children's banter unsettling and was glad when the dishes had been cleared. Sarah offered a pie for dessert and John graciously accepted. Dessert was not offered to the children as the older children dutifully took their younger siblings up to the cabin loft. John fumbled with his fork as he tried to enjoy his pie in the presence of an unmarried woman. Sarah led the conversation about moving from Virginia and the contrasts between Kentucky life and living in Virginia. She loved the beautiful Bluegrass country, picking wild berries, growing a garden in the rich soil and the friendly sense of community on the frontier. John nodded and appreciated her positive outlook given her desperate situation. How could anyone be so strong and positive in this circumstance? As their conversation became more unguarded and relaxed, Sarah asked about John's future in hunting and trapping. John spoke enthusiastically about the growing market for fur on the Ohio and how the French were paying higher prices for pelts. Sarah could hear in John's voice the excitement and passion enjoyed in his life and her hopes for their lives together were dashed. She expressed her admiration for his hunting prowess and all that he had done for her and her family. In a final effort to draw him into her family, Sarah reached across the table to hold John's hand offering her loneliness and asking John "if he felt lonely those many days in the woods."

It was with great relief and some regret that Colter learned the Boones were taking a group of Kentuckians back to Virginia and the Davis family would be traveling with them. John's mother was most disappointed, as she hoped Sarah Davis would be the answer to her prayers for John. Now her son was having success with his hunting and trapping business and living in the village when he was not trading furs on the Ohio River in Maysville. Her concern for her son grew when he told her that he had joined the Kentucky militia to stop the Indian and British incursions and the many attacks occurring on the frontier.

The Northwest Territory spanned Ohio to the headwaters of the Mississippi River and it had been a political pawn in an international chess match. The term "all politics are local" applied in this region with multiple indigenous communities fighting other communities to hold territory and commercial advantages. The French, British and now the Americans entered these local struggles with their own agenda, their iron trading goods and the power of their weaponry. While Kentucky had been the scene of intense conflict between Americans moving west and indigenous communities, the center of conflict shifted north of the Ohio River. After the American Revolutionary War, the Treaty of Paris ceded the Northwest Territory to the United States of America. The apparent resolution of who controlled this area was just the beginning of some vicious fights, as the indigenous communities were not party to the treaty. To make matter worse, the British sought to continue their presence in the region and the American settlers moving into the area were outside the protection and laws of the new United States of America. The Northwest Ordinance passed by Congress in 1787 had established the federal government as the sovereign entity to control settlement and relations with the indigenous communities. This ambitious legislation established territorial government, land rights and education, among other laws, but most important to the indigenous peoples was the clause establishing "their lands and property shall never be taken from them without their consent." The movement of settlers into the lands north of the Ohio was not only encroachment into tribal lands, but violations of U.S. law.

Having been pushed out of their native lands to the east by European settlers, many indigenous communities were determined to make their stand in the woodlands of Ohio and Indiana. The Shawnee were seemingly a people without a home. In one of the great ironies of the European push into Kentucky was the fact that the Shawnee had once called the Shenandoah Valley, West Virginia and Pennsylvania "home." Having been pushed into Kentucky and Ohio, the Shawnee were once again challenged by European settlements and conflict. To strengthen their position, the Shawnee allied with the remnants of the Iroquois, Wabash, Miami, Illini, Wyandot, Menominee, Kickapoo, Cherokee and Muscogee; this became known as the Western Confederacy. The newly elected president, George Washington, had himself fought the French and Indians in the Northwest Territory and now had a growing concern about the power of the Western Confederacy of tribes.

As the Western Confederacy became more aggressive and violent toward the wave of settlers moving into Kentucky and Ohio, President Washington directed the military to take action. The first effort involved local militia under General Josiah Harmar who was defeated by the Western Confederacy. The second effort was nothing short of a massacre as Major General Arthur St. Clair marched his combined regular and militia forces into the worst defeat of the U.S. army, losing 632 of his 920 men. The new republic disbanded most of its professional military after the Revolutionary War, but now the Western Confederacy with British support threatened U.S. sovereignty over the Northwest Territory. Washington convinced Congress that a professional army was needed on the frontier to meet this threat and turned to one of his most trusted commanders in the Revolutionary War, General Anthony Wayne, to build a force capable of defeating the Confederacy. Wayne formed four brigades consisting of musket infantry, a rifle battalion, horse-mounted dragoons and artillery. He knew his fight would be in woodland territory and most likely involve combat in close quarters. Wayne spent months training and drilling his recruits, including extensive training with bayonet and musket. He built a force of several thousand, but requested additional troops to meet the expected enemy forces in Ohio. Having completed training near Pittsburgh he moved his army down the Ohio River and disembarked at Cincinnati for their foray into Western Confederacy territory. Wayne concluded that previous efforts to defeat the Confederacy relied too heavily on undisciplined militia, so now he had a fighting army that would avoid the defeats of the past. The Kentucky militia had an equal disdain for the regular army and had success in previous campaigns against the Indians using quick, mounted attacks on villages usually in retribution for an attack by marauding Indians seeking horses and, at times, white scalps.

Upon arrival in Cincinnati, Wayne learned that the additional forces he needed would not be provided, as recruitment was lagging expectations. His only option was to recruit additional forces from local militia, the very thing he wanted to avoid. Wayne wanted to engage the enemy before winter started in the Ohio region, so he had little time to supplement his regular troops with militia. Secretary of War Henry Knox turned to a Revolutionary War officer, General Charles Scott, who had moved to the frontier. The governor of the newly formed state of Kentucky chose Scott to lead the state militia before Secretary of War Knox commissioned Scott as Major General over the Kentucky militia. Scott knew many of the experienced Indian fighters in Kentucky and was known better than Simon Kenton. Kenton was a natural leader, an opportunist, a risk taker, an adopted son of the Shawnee, a charismatic rounder, a frontier individualist. Unlike the Boones who created a farming community and managed the risks of the frontier, Kenton was a risk taker who operated solo. The Boones extolled the benefits of community, while Kenton was the individualist. The Boones were predictable, while Kenton was an adventurer. Kenton was the kind of man that John Colter admired. Kenton owned land above Maysville on the Ohio River in Kentucky and sold the land to businessmen arriving down the Ohio who sought to conduct river commerce. Whether it be iron pots, knives, muskets, furs, whiskey, or sewing needles, the area's mercantile houses traded for goods or for currency. John Colter often brought his skins and furs to the growing community newly named Washington, Kentucky. Colter seldom saw Kenton, but heard many stories of this frontier legend. While Kenton was a fierce fighter, well acquainted with the Indians of the area, he did not possess an understanding of military tactics or discipline.

When Colter heard that Kenton was forming a militia company, he was interested, as was his friend Forrest Hancock. While in Maysville, they visited the encampment of militia being formed by Kenton and learned of the detachment's mission and its role and compensation for joining Wayne's forces. As militia joining the regular army of Wayne, they would receive a wage lower than the professional army's wage but would receive an advance of $10. They would provide their own weapons, horses, ammunition, clothing and shelter. By law no militia man could be compelled to serve more than three months. The Kentucky militia owned a proud tradition, including many skirmishes and battles with indigenous peoples and the British. Many of the men gathered on the Ohio River had previously fought in these battles and both fathers of Colter and Hancock fought in the militia, so the two sons now joined in the long-standing effort to make the frontier safe for settlers' families. Each man in the Kentucky militia had a clear self-interest in pushing back the tribes of the Western Confederacy and willingly joined Wayne's efforts. At the same time, each member of the militia viewed the regular army with suspicion as the new federal government often used the standing army in the Northwest Territory to drive squatters off public domain and to protect Indian treaty rights. In addition, the previous professional army generals had led their armies to disaster in the Ohio wilderness.

Many of the Kentucky militia were farmers and not as accomplished with the long rifle nor as capable on a horse as the two young hunters. During target practice it became apparent that Colter and Hancock were excellent marksmen and as such would be among those designated to hunt for game that would feed the militia. There was little time for much training other than forming ranks, target practice and procuring supplies for the journey north. Colter, Hancock and the Kentucky militia traveled down the Ohio River to Fort Washington at Cincinnati where they joined Wayne's forces. Wayne ordered Scott and the Kentucky militia to attack some Indian villages some one hundred miles from Fort Washington with nine hundred men. The militia refused given the time of year and the likelihood they would be outnumbered two to one. Colter and Hancock listened to their fellow Kentuckians talk about the incompetent regular army, so they joined most of the Kentuckians in their exodus from Fort Washington. Not only was there a consensus that Wayne did not understand frontier tactics, but most needed to return for the harvest. Soon General Scott joined his departing volunteers, hoping that the spring movement on the Indians would generate a greater commitment by the Kentucky militia.

During the remaining days of 1793 and winter of 1794, things worsened for Wayne and his relationship with the Kentuckians. When told of the militia refusals and their return to Kentucky, Secretary Knox withheld payment for the militia services. After much pressure from Scott and Wayne and ultimately President Washington, the militia was paid, with hopes of attracting them back in the spring. In addition, while Wayne's army wintered at Fort Washington, numerous Indian raids were conducted across the Ohio River. One such raid occurred near Maysville where thirty-six horses were stolen by Indians and another raid in Harrison County resulted in the deaths of two settlers. Colter joined a group of thirty Mason County residents wanting to retrieve their horses. Like most raids, it was apparent to Colter that no more than five Indians stole these horses. Their trail led to a popular crossing of the Ohio and Colter figured they were less than one day ahead of them and would be slowed trying to drive that many horses. In addition, driving that many horses could only be accomplished on a trail wide enough to accommodate horses and their new masters, so tracking was no problem. The third day into the pursuit, the Kentuckians caught up with the thieves and their horses in a meadow where horses were foraging and the Indians were preparing for the night. Colter was told to go with fifteen other men to the far side of the meadow where they would intercept horse and Indian as the remaining members would attack from their current position. After being properly positioned, the attack began, with horses and Indians sent running in all directions. Colter remained mounted to trap horses and secure an advantage over an escaping Indian. As horse and Indian ran toward him, he spotted an Indian running between two horses. Colter urged his horse toward the threesome and could see that the Indian could be no more than sixteen years of age with a face painted for raiding. Colter took full advantage of his mounted position as he fell upon the lad with his rifle still strapped to his back and knife drawn which plunged into the Indian's throat. The remaining Indian raiders disappeared into the forest, but all the horses were recovered and returned to Maysville. Upon their return, Maysville's residents wanted to hear of Colter's attack and the success of the pursuit. There was also a father who had come from Harrison County to inquire if the dead Indian owned a scalp that might have been his son's. Colter was sad to say no scalp was possessed by the Indian.

As spring arrived, Wayne began nervously waiting to hear from Scott and his recruiting results. Wayne wanted to engage the enemy by September and it was not until late July that Scott delivered fifteen hundred Kentucky militia for the journey north of the Ohio River. Wayne arranged his forces to cover his flanks and deploy reconnaissance using militia and Chickasaw and Choctaw scouts. Wayne's plan was to move toward the British fort and indigenous communities near Lake Erie and to build forts along the trail to ensure supply, hold territory and provide safe harbor.

Several days into the journey, Colter was riding ahead of the van hunting deer, which were plentiful in the woodlands. As he traveled he came upon a sight that became seared into his memory. It was a scene of chaos and debris. Strewn across the clearing were blankets, tents, saddles, cooking utensils, clothing, cannon and the drying bones of men and horses. The crashing silence of a lost battle and death brought Colter down from his saddle as he carefully navigated between skeletons and the instruments of everyday life on the trail. Most disturbing to Colter were the crushed skulls, open crying jaws and oddly angled arms and legs of the dead. Colter stood in the midst of St. Clair's debacle. The buckskin clothing rotting on the ground jabbed Colter's confidence and sense of invincibility. He had always depended on his skills and decisions to survive on the frontier, but now he was exposed to the decisions and skills of another eastern general pushing toward the very forces that had left the chaos that was before his eyes. Colter walked his horse to the edge of the clearing and escaped away in the wood heading back to the militia traveling on Wayne's left flank.

Colter found Hancock riding along the edge of the militia caravan. Hancock was shocked by the look on Colter's face of horror and regret. The two rode silently side by side until Hancock asked where Colter had been. Colter was not given to hyperbole or drama, but on this occasion he told Hancock that he had been to "hell." Colter shared his distrust of Wayne's plan and the doom that lay in wait in the woodlands before them. These comments from a man who had never expressed fear or regret caused Hancock to stop his horse. They both had heard of the St. Clair slaughter, but had dismissed it as misfortune for the whites and luck for the clueless Indians. Now it was apparent that the foe was not clueless and was perhaps more cunning than the uniformed leaders of their expedition. Hancock was the first to mention slipping off into the woods and returning to Kentucky. Desertion was a daily occurrence among the regular army and the militia, and being part of the militia the penalty would be slight if any. As they discussed their situation word came down through the ranks that the army would be moving into a clearing ahead filled with the remnants of St. Clair's army where they would bury the bones of the defeated and build a fort. Wayne wanted to bury the futility of the past while establishing his strength for all to see along the trail. This boldness and confidence encouraged Colter and Hancock to remain, but to keep their options open. A quick retreat into a fort to their rear sounded like a good plan. Wayne named the new construction "Fort Recovery" and this sounded good to Colter who was starting to like the confidence of Wayne. Simon Kenton also liked Wayne's style. Simon Kenton knew the Shawnee better than anyone, having been captured and adopted by them. Kenton respected the Shawnee people and their desire for a homeland, but he also understood that they had allied themselves with the diminishing British remaining in the Northwest Territory. The frontier was no place for misplaced alliances and wishes to keep things as they had been. Wayne constructed two more forts as he pushed closer to the Confederacy stronghold and British fort.

Colter knew they were closing on the enemy, but his duties of hunting and meat provisions kept him away from the main body of Wayne's van. On a hot August day Colter was following a deer trace that promised a successful hunt. While his hunting skills served the militia with a regular diet of fresh meat, his concern grew for firing his long rifle in earshot of the enemy. Following the deer trace, he smelled then saw the rising smoke from a small collection of birch bark houses forming a village of Shawnee. To his right, he noted a field of maize maturing in the summer sun. Colter dismounted and began his reconnaissance of the village. There were five houses, eight females engaged in drying meat, two older men talking by the smoking fire and several children playing some type of game unfamiliar to Colter. Colter knew that there were other males residing in this village, but where could they be? As Colter watched the children play he thought of young Joshua Davis somewhere in Virginia.

After watching this sublime scene, Colter left his clearing and retraced his steps down the deer trace that had led him to the village. If Wayne's van fell upon this village of five houses, there would be instant destruction and death for the innocent. Colter did not appreciate the Shawnee sedentary life, but he pondered the future of the children playing their game. They were so innocent and ignorant of the force moving upon them and their way of life. Unlike Joshua Davis, they would not have the option of returning to a safe haven.

Wayne's advance guard of Chickasaw encountered heavy resistance from a sheltered enemy among trees felled by a storm that left trees prone on the ground and ready made for defense. Colter and Hancock were well to the left of this engagement and heard musket fire in the distance. The advance guard reported to Wayne's officers that a large force was in their front. Wayne wanted to see for himself, so he mounted his horse wearing the singular uniform of the army general in command and moved forward to the sound of muskets. The heat of August rested upon Wayne's regulars, but not one blue coat had been removed. Wayne's infantry bayonets were shining in the sun as he pushed his infantry into the fight. His elite rifle unit slipped into the rear of the Indians now retreating in front of the infantry charge. The rifle unit, which included William Clark, started picking off the retreating Indian fighters as they ran toward the cover of the British fort in their rear.

Colter and Hancock were holding their horses as the gunfire intensified and the roar of an infantry bayonet charge could be heard over the field of battle. They then thought they heard the order "charge," which unleashed their horses as they ran toward the sound of battle. The fallen trees and smoke drifting over the scene engulfed Colter and Hancock. Moving as if being sucked into battle, the horses started jumping over tree trunks. Hancock's horse stumbled over a large cottonwood causing him to fall among the tree trunks. Colter spotted an enemy warrior running to his left and took aim with his one shot, which had little effect on the young man running for his life and disappearing into the woods.

Colter then turned to see that Hancock was lying beneath a large Indian who was drawing his knife. Colter kicked his horse to advance on the two combatants and yelled to gain the Indian's attention, at which point Colter's tomahawk found its mark in the shoulder of the Indian. As the wounded Indian rolled over in pain, Hancock's knife quickly entered the Indian's abdomen just below his breast bone. And then it was over. In just sixty minutes, the Western Confederacy had been defeated and driven back to the British fort where the doors remained closed and the British and Indian power north of the Ohio River was broken.

Wayne gathered his wounded and celebrated the victory by taunting the British hiding behind their stockade. After several days of revelry in front of the British fort and destroying Indian villages, Wayne ordered his army to begin moving back toward Fort Recovery. As the Kentucky militia moved along Wayne's flank, it came upon a small village of five birch bark houses. The militia stormed into the village knocking over drying racks, fire pots and buckskin chairs as the women and children started running into the woods. Colter did not join the charge as he watched a horse trample a six-year-old boy who was running for his life. Several of the old men of the village ran in among the militia and pulled two Kentuckians to the ground only to be crumpled by tomahawk blows to the head. As Colter rode away, the sweet smoke of drying meat had been replaced by the pungent odor of burning birch wood and the corn that was ripe for harvesting. The Shawnee once again had no home.

Colter and Hancock rode beside men older than they, men who built homes from logs, men who turned the virgin soil, men who had buried children and men who faced the depredations of the frontier weather and Indian marauders. Two such men were Jonathan Clark and Amos Page. They met during the construction of Fort Recovery. The Kentuckians were tasked with downing trees for the stockade, while the regular troops of Wayne placed the logs and mudded the gaps. Colter and Hancock could handle musket and knife, but compared to Clark and Page they were amateurs with axe and saw. As the men labored, Clark challenged Colter and Hancock with the bet he could fell four trees in the time it took them to fell two trees together. They refused the whiskey bet but accepted a bet of dried beef. Clark enjoyed his extra portion of dried beef and never let Colter and Hancock forget their futile effort to match his skill with an axe. While Clark and Page won the respect of the two hunters handling the axe, Colter and Hancock had won most of the shooting contests and Colter's conduct on the field of battle impressed and inspired Clark and Page.

As they rode back toward the Ohio River, the four shared their Kentucky stories and their hopes and aspirations for the future. Jonathan Clark had brought his young wife and two children through the Allegheny Mountains hoping to secure land in Mercer County Kentucky. Upon arrival with five other families, the Clarks laid claim to ten acres along a creek and started clearing land. It was early summer and they were confident that a corn crop could be grown by October and a garden could produce the beans and squash to feed their children. In August, these plans were upset by an agent of Thomas Durham showing documents proving that this land was not their land. They pleaded with the agent for the opportunity to rent and purchase the land, but to no avail. After threatening legal action under the laws of Virginia which had jurisdiction, they negotiated one year's rent to make the harvest and shelter for the winter then move elsewhere. The next spring, the Clarks left the cleared land and cabin and moved to Harrison County where they negotiated to buy ten acres of land with five years of hard work. Amos Page was a neighbor of Clarks as was Page's brother. It was the misfortune of Page that his brother was traveling from his home to help Amos finish building a barn. On this journey, three Shawnee fell upon him to take his horse and his scalp. Amos was filled with anger and a driving need for revenge against all Indians. The shedding of blood by individuals whether they be Indian or white created enmity against all of the enemy race. Even though Page and Clark had families to care for and a harvest to reap in the fall, they dedicated themselves to punish Indians for their transgressions. The victory at Fallen Timbers secured a new level of safety for their families in Kentucky, but Page's anger and bitterness were as fierce as ever.

The Page and Clark families shared an important link in the form of Pastor John Ray who was a Methodist preacher of some note in Northern Kentucky. Ray was a large man standing over six feet tall and weighing 250 pounds. His wit, intelligence and biting sarcasm surpassed his physical presence as an itinerant Methodist preacher who could humble a Baptist in three sentences and inspire a seeker with even fewer words. Ray fearlessly traveled the counties of Northern Kentucky by himself, which inspired those living in fear of Indian marauders. As there was not a church building, Ray preached in the homes of the believers and seekers. Due to the Indian threats, most Kentuckians lived in homes clustered near a blockhouse or fort, so Ray could preach to many seekers in one location. The Page and Clark families had Baptist histories in Virginia, but now belonged to the growing Methodist community in Northern Kentucky. Ray visited every two weeks when he would deliver a sermon followed by an open sharing of challenges to a healthy soul and the wonders of the inner life. This discussion was followed by a dinner where the families discussed the fear, isolation and occasional heartbreak of the frontier adventure. Jonathan Clark asked Colter if he knew of Ray or had ever attended a worship service on the frontier. John related that his father owned a Bible, said grace before every meal and the family had attended some preacher gatherings in a neighbor's house, but he had no recollection of the details. Colter knew where this conversation was heading and wanted to avoid the inevitable invitation, so he baited Clark with the statement that God seemed to keep his distance from those on the frontier and everyone else for that matter. Clark responded with a favorite reference to Moses and the Hebrews wandering in the wilderness until they settled in a land surrounded by enemies. Clark went on to state that God was among the frontier settlers as Jesus was with them always. Colter grunted at that comment and retorted that he had traveled many miles in Northern Kentucky and had never seen Jesus. Clark jumped in and said he should attend the next gathering of the Methodists as John Ray brings Jesus with him every time. Colter's plan had failed and there was the invitation. Hancock had been a spectator to this exchange on horseback and chuckled at Colter's defeat.

Not long after they arrived at Fort Recovery, the Kentucky mounted volunteers began to demand a discharge and payment for their services. It was harvest time and the men knew their wives and children would be working long days to harvest the beans, squash and corn followed by efforts to preserve the food and store it for the winter. General Scott knew the three months of service was nearing completion for his volunteers and had seen volunteers just leave without proper discharge in previous campaigns. Scott was proud of his Kentuckians and wanted a proper discharge and payment to ensure a proper and respectful separation from Wayne's Regulars. There would be more battles to fight and future need of joining the Regular army to the Kentucky volunteers, so a proper separation was important. Scott accomplished his goal and his men began their journeys back to their communities in Kentucky as proud residents of the newest state in the United States of America. Page and Clark enjoyed an outpouring of love and relief from their families as they rode into their compound. Colter and Hancock separated as Hancock returned to his family farm and Colter walked into his cold and empty rented room in the hills above the Ohio River.

CHAPTER FOUR
Pushing Back the Unknown

The warmth of the Clatsop hut and Colter's young woman companion were welcome changes from the hellacious chores of pushing, rowing, walking and riding twenty-one hundred miles from Camp Dubois and the incessant rain and cold of the Northwest coastal winter. After the thrill of waking each morning not knowing where food or camp would be found, Fort Clatsop was almost unbearable. The journey of the Corps of Discovery became most arduous after the whiskey supply ran out at the Great Falls, the hunting became sparse, the mountain snow unbearable and the hunger painful. Colter thought things could not get worse, but they did. At Fort Clatsop, Lewis and Clark instituted a strict military routine for the winter quarters. This was not in Colter's nature as he was a hunter accustomed to the freedom of the hunt and the thrill of the unseen and the unexpected. He particularly did not like being posted on guard duty nor did he enjoy sharing small quarters with five other men. Now on the third day of a "hunt" he was enjoying the warmth of a Clatsop hut and the body of a woman who had earned some of Colter's tobacco.

Colter knew the Clatsop and Mandan Indians and found them to be gracious and curious people. They were not as hostile to outsiders as many of the tribes and villages. The Clatsop had more visits from whites traveling the ocean and the Columbia River and with that interaction came some bargaining skills and acquisitiveness not seen on the Missouri River. What made these two distant peoples similar was their respect for the Great Spirit and their regard for all things that supported their survival. Whether it was the buffalo or the Salmon, the blueberry or the beans, the grass or the tree, all these living things were part of the Great Spirit's blessing and each living thing had a unique spirit that endeared it to the Clatsop and the Mandan. As Colter lay in the warm hut, he wondered what spirit he carried with him in the eyes of his companion. To him, she was on object of desire and she sold herself for a bit of tobacco. Thinking of her as a fellow human being equal to him was not possible. At the very best, she was a child-human and at worst she was an opportunist living as the animals lived. He knew enough of the language to learn that her name meant Sandpiper Woman or Skookum Klootch. This derisive name only reinforced his thinking of the Indians as being closer to animals than humans, as being objects to either facilitate or impede the desires of the whites. To the Clatsop village, Skookum Klootch suggested an energetic, strong person who could be found in many places. Skookum Klootch was widely respected for her ability to catch salmon with her salmon traps and nets and her ability to feed her father's family. She did not enjoy cooking and sewing, which made her different from her sisters, but she gained great respect from her father for her fishing abilities. Skookum Klootch revered her father and sought out trading opportunities with the whites to gain gifts for him. In the case of Colter, tobacco would be much appreciated by the father of Skookum Klootch.

Colter did not understand the motives of Skookum Klootch nor did he understand the value that the Clatsop placed on the objects brought by the whites. What he did understand was the collective warmth and harmony of the Clatsop village. In this moist forest setting, the Clatsop lived a collective life of freedom from want, freedom from hunger, freedom from threats and freedom from a drive to achieve. Colter harbored disdain for the males in the Clatsop village who spent hours playing games, smoking and talking nonsense about life's mysteries. Catching fish was woman's work in the village, so what was left for the men of the village? There were no hostile neighbors and the salmon swam to the village every year, so the men played their games, smoked their tobacco and made idle talk. It occurred to Colter that Skookum Klootch was more akin to his life as she was a provider; she had precious few idle hours and her family depended on her. How could he think of her so coldly? She gave herself to Colter for his pleasure. Colter was the taker;

she was the giver. Colter felt shame as he knew the provider carried a quiet burden. How many times had he returned to camp after days harvesting meat for the Corps with little appreciation or respect? This brief regret preceded a sound sleep lying under bear fur while the fire provided warmth and the familiar sounds of a crackling wood fire.

Colter awoke to the smell of seared meat and cooked balsamroot. Lying next to the bear fur was an ample meal prepared for him and sitting across the hut's small room was Skookum Klootch watching Colter awake from his sleep and discover the meal she had prepared for him. Startled by her generosity, his regret returned as he saw the provider waiting to witness his enjoyment of her provision. His regret quickly gave way to his hunger pangs and the allure of the meal sitting before him. Colter devoured the elk meat that provided a welcome change from the salmon and venison he and the Corps had been eating. What Colter did not appreciate was the trade that Skookum Klootch had made for the elk meat using some of the tobacco she had earned from Colter. She was the master of the salmon, not the elk, but she understood what Colter wanted most.

Colter and Skookum Klootch continued their encounters in the weeks following until Colter's tobacco supply was depleted. Colter considered his dilemma and wondered about his prospects in returning to Skookum Klootch's hut without the requisite tobacco. He decided to make his visit without the tobacco and see what would transpire. Having gained entry into the small room of the Clatsop hut he began his advances without offering the tobacco and received a quick rebuke. This startled him as he had imagined that his company had gained him access without a trade of goods or payment. Whether Skookum Klootch shared his desire for another encounter without tobacco, Colter would never know. This affront caused Colter to become angry and as he stood up on the bear fur he showed his anger and stormed out of the hut charging past the cooked elk meat and cooked balsamroot that had been prepared for him whether he brought tobacco or not.

Lewis and the men of the Corps had had enough of the winter in these parts. Lewis and Clark thought their provisions adequate to start their return to Saint Louis with one major provision lacking and that was enough canoe capacity to get the Corps to the mountains. The Clatsop canoes were not only functionally excellent, but they were works of art and a source of tribal identity and pride. No other tribes encountered by Lewis and Clark could surpass the quality of the Clatsop canoe. Lewis made multiple offers to the Clatsop for their canoes and each time was rebuffed by a counter offer that seemed excessive to Lewis. Most of the trading goods with which Lewis and Clark started in Saint Louis had been given or traded, so what remained was very dear to Lewis for their return trip. Lewis was impatient to start moving up the Columbia, so he decided he would do something he had vowed never to do on this journey and that was to steal from the Indians. Lewis devised a plan to invite a Clatsop chief to his quarters and entertain him while his men would steal one of the long Clatsop canoes and hide it until the day of the Corps' departure. The plan worked to perfection. As the Corps began its push against the current of the Columbia, the Clatsop took possession of Fort Clatsop and its few remaining articles while the Corps of Discovery started its journey home. Skookum Klootch ran to the abandoned fort with the others as word spread that the visitors had departed. By the time she arrived, little was left to scavenge. Running to the fort had brought on a nausea that was getting more frequent, especially in the morning. She ran to a corner of the fort where she vomited and regretted coming all this way for nothing.

Once again, the men were pushing against the river current as they negotiated the Columbia River. The hunting and fishing had been adequate to sustain them for several days, but the food supplies would need to be supplemented as they moved toward the Rockies once again. The scarcity of food and the harsh conditions found in the Rockies were fresh in the minds of each man. In addition, there was uncertainty regarding the horses they would need when their canoes no longer would suffice for their transportation. Coming west for the first time, no one could anticipate the hardships nor know the requirements of survival. Now going back east over familiar hardships, the men knew what was needed to survive.

Another difference from their last foray into the Rockies was the emergence of distinct roles, expectations and relationships. Hunger could be solved only by food, food could only be acquired by hunting and hunting was done best by George Drouillard. A hungry man can look past many differences and suspicions. Drouillard's differences from the other members of the Corps were significant, but they diminished with each deer, elk and bear he killed. The men of the Corps depended on his hunting skills and Lewis and Clark depended on his translating skills and good sense in dealing with the Indians. Drouillard was not enlisted in the Corps and he traveled as a civilian, so had a freedom not enjoyed by the other members. It was to his credit that Drouillard took orders from Lewis and Clark very well. He was as invested and committed to the success of the Corps as any man, which garnered him more respect, given his unique status. Given his status as a private citizen, he was free to trade with the Indians and whites on his own account. He owned his own traps and when possible he trapped and sold beaver and otter for his own gain.

The Fields brothers and several members of the Corps thought of Drouillard as invincible. Being younger members of the Corps, they looked up to George for guidance and leadership as did several other younger members of the Corps. John Colter was the same age as Drouillard. He resented the adoration given Drouillard even though his hunting success had been comparable during the western trek to the Pacific. The difference was Drouillard's presence, his confidence, his worldliness and his influence with the younger Corps members and the Frenchmen he recruited to the Corps. Colter possessed equal hunting skills, but not the attractive personality of George Drouillard. Colter's world had been limited to the Kentucky frontier while Drouillard's father was a man of great influence among Indians and Europeans alike throughout the Northwest Territory and Canada. Colter knew how to survive in the forest while Drouillard knew how to survive in the world of clashing tribes, countries and cultures.

Colter's jealousy and distaste for Drouillard grew over the winter at Fort Clatsop. The confined quarters of Fort Clatsop were stifling, so the men sought the enjoyment of games, storytelling and social engagement. Drouillard excelled at frontier games, telling harrowing stories and engaging the younger members of the Corps with good natured bragging. Colter was the man in the corner of the room. He despised the evenings around the fire at Fort Clatsop. To make matters worse, his hunting success was meager in the forests surrounding Fort Clatsop while Drouillard was having good success hunting with the Fields brothers.

While Colter suffered in Drouillard's shadow over the winter, he did appreciate the growing confidence placed in him by William Clark. The fellow Kentuckian took note of Colter's quiet successes in hunting and tracking and his courage during their westward journey. Clark selected Colter for special assignments, which most recently was the difficult journey over the coastal mountain range to establish a salt-making station on the Pacific Coast. The respect was mutual. Clark was five years senior to Colter, but many more years advanced in knowledge of the larger world of politics, economics and the ability to lead men. Colter understood this and greatly respected the fact that Clark never acted superior to Colter and treated him with the respect he sought. Clark chose to leave his family's land holdings and their agricultural business to join the push of America into the frontier waiting to be understood and tamed. In a way, Colter had made the same decision to leave his father's farm and roam the frontier for pelts and discovery. Colter wanted to be part of this push and Clark was the type of man he wanted to follow. Lewis was too distant and isolated while Clark understood the collective effort needed to push into the west.

Six weeks into the eastward trek toward the mountains, Colter and Drouillard clashed. The food supplies of Fort Clatsop and the meat garnered by Drouillard and the Fields brothers had been depleted as the men pushed up the Columbia River. As the Corps approached the mountains, they were once again facing the uncertainties of adequate transportation and food. The deer, elk, salmon and bear that supplied their food needs was now greatly diminished. Not even the great hunter Drouillard could bring enough meat to the Corps to satisfy its hunger for protein. The only source of protein in this region was the Indians, who themselves were fighting hunger. Lewis and Clark bargained if not begged for the scarce protein the Indians could provide in the forms of horse meat and dog meat. This was an embarrassment to the hunters in the Corps who took their role of providers very seriously.

The Indians of this region suffered from a serious eye condition that

Clark called "sore eyes" and Clark had an antidote that helped treat the "sore eyes" condition. Clark took Drouillard with him to the village to negotiate for horse meat and brought Colter along as well. Drouillard's sign language was useful as always and the deal was struck. Clark treated several Indians with sore eyes, including the chief's wife, and received in return a wild, unbroken horse. As the chief offered the horse reins to Drouillard, Colter took the reins and began leading the horse back to the encampment. Drouillard felt slighted and reached to take the reins from Colter. To Colter, leading three hundred pounds of horse meat into the encampment was worth fighting for. It was Clark who had procured the horse, not Drouillard. Colter was determined to keep Drouillard from claiming success in gaining meat for the men that he was unable to provide from his hunting efforts. As Drouillard grabbed for the reins, Colter put his shoulder into Drouillard's mid-section, which was quickly followed by a mighty left hand to Colter's chin. Colter dropped like a leaf. Clark was stunned by this quick turn of events. Two men he respected the most in the Corps of Discovery were now about to kill each other. As Drouillard and Colter drew their knives for combat, Clark stepped in front of Colter, knowing that Drouillard would make quick work of the smaller and less accomplished knife fighter. As Drouillard's knife flashed past Clark's face, Clark turned on Drouillard and with a swift kick sent Drouillard's knife flying into the air. It was over as quickly as it had begun and the prized horse ran off into the valley never to be seen again.

This brief encounter left Colter feeling embarrassed and not a part of the Corps of Discovery. He knew word would get back to the rest of the Corps and Drouillard's followers would now see Colter in a different light. Colter also felt bad that this incident occurred in Clark's presence. Colter had started badly with the Corps at Camp Dubois, but earned the respect of most of the Corps, including William Clark, whom Colter idolized and aspired to emulate. Clark was not a bombast like Drouillard and earned the respect of the Corps with his steady leadership and respectful approach to each person of the Corps. Clark took particular care of the young Indian mother, Sacagawea and her young son, who had jointed the Corps at Fort Mandan as a translator and guide. Clark felt no compulsion to brag or hold his esteemed family name over anyone. His quiet frontier humility was shared by Colter, but now Colter knew his relationship with the Corps and Clark had been changed. Colter's standing and self-esteem suffered another blow when he and his horse stumbled into a small river in the Bitterroot Mountains. With the spring snow melt in full force, Colter's horse slipped as they traversed the river and the current pushed man and beast down the river until they could "regain their legs" near a riverbank shallows. While tumbling down the river, Colter lost some of his gear, but managed to hold onto his rifle. Colter emerged from the water bruised and sore, but neither he nor his horse sustained any broken bones. As Colter walked his horse down the riverbank looking for a crossing point back to the Corps' train, insults and comments rained down on him from Corps members, especially from the Fields brothers.

Lewis and Clark wanted to explore more of the rivers to the east of the Bitterroot Mountains. To accomplish this, the captains developed a plan that would require the Corps to be split into several groups after they emerged from the treacherous Bitterroot Mountains. Lewis would take nine men and travel north to explore the Marias and other rivers feeding into the Missouri River. Clark would take twenty men, fifty horses and Sacajawea with her son down to the Jefferson River where they would retrieve the cache of supplies and canoes they had left the previous fall. Having done this, Clark would then split his group into a group taking supplies down the Missouri River and Clark with the remaining Corps would travel to the Yellowstone River. Colter was assigned to Ordway's group to take the canoes down the Missouri to the Great Falls where they would meet most of the Lewis contingent. Since Colter served under Ordway, it was normal that he would be assigned to the canoe group, but Colter was now overly sensitive and felt that his horsemanship skills were seen as inadequate. Colter was glad to see that Drouillard and the Fields brothers departed with Lewis. Colter did not know that Ordway had insisted on taking Colter because of his excellent canoe skills and his hunting ability. While Colter and Ordway had had a rough start at Camp Dubois, Ordway now held Colter in high regard. He still did not much like him, but he respected Colter's effectiveness as a provider for the Corps and his steely nerve to hunt far away from the main body of the Corps in unknown and hostile territory. As for Colter, he respected Ordway's New England sturdiness and willingness to take on the hard tasks of the Corp and appreciated the fact that Ordway gave him more slack as the journey progressed.

Ordway's group enjoyed their trip down the Missouri as hunting was good, the river was swift and the evening gatherings were lively as the accomplishments and challenges of the last two years were shamelessly embellished. Colter enjoyed the company of these men and the beauty of the high bluffs and green rolling hills of the land. Hunting without a horse, Colter could track his prey on foot and use the draws and ravines to cover his approach and gain a clean shot at his target. Traveling with a small group, Colter was no longer required to hunt with a partner as had been required by Clark after several grizzly bear attacks. These bears proved they could continue a charge after taking several wounds from a rifle, so a single shot had to be a head shot or a single hunter would be the loser in any encounter with a grizzly. Colter had been charged once during the journey in an area not too far from the route he was now taking, but Colter's confidence in his rifle skill did not deter him from walking in prime grizzly country where game was abundant.

When Ordway's group arrived at the Great Falls, Ordway chose Colter to guide one of the two canoes that would traverse the dangerous white water, while the rest of the men would portage around the falls. Perched in the canoe's stern and with a canoe full of supplies, Colter took the lead of the two canoes as they were pushed by the high and rapid flow of the Missouri. As the lead, Colter needed to plan his route based on his quick assessment of the rocks, tree snags and sand bars that were visible and invisible. The canoe's speed increased as the channel narrowed and the rapids boiled. The sound of thousands of gallons of water crashing into rocks was deafening and added to the white-knuckle grip on Colter's paddle. Keeping the bow pointed downstream was critical and using the force of the water to keep the bow true was best done by not slowing the canoe and by using the paddle as a rudder only. As Colter's canoe shot out of the last rapids, Ordway and his men gave a loud hoo-ha and fired guns in celebration.

Meanwhile, Lewis took Drouillard and the Fields brothers up the Marias River to explore an area bypassed on their previous visit to the area. Riding their horses along the river, the four men encountered eight Blackfeet Indians. After the salutations translated by Drouillard, the eight Blackfeet insisted on spending the night camped with Lewis and his three companions. During the night, Joseph Fields woke Lewis, Drouillard and his brother with a scream that warned the others, who quickly realized that their rifles were in the Blackfeet hands and their horses were about to be stolen. Fields flew at one Indian pushing his knife into his chest and retrieving his rifle while Lewis grabbed his rifle from another Indian and shot with his pistol another Indian who was stealing his horse. The aggressive assault by the four visitors put the remaining Blackfeet into a full retreat giving time for Lewis and his three men to begin their gallop to the Missouri River where they joined Ordway's group.

Colter's days in the canoe afforded him time to start thinking about his return to Saint Louis. He wanted no part of Saint Louis and the growing city on the Mississippi. The hunting and trapping in Kentucky did not compare to the opportunities witnessed during the last two years. After his absence from Kentucky, he could only imagine how much land was now controlled by settlers and farmers and how much more depleted the wild game would be. He considered returning to Kentucky to see his blood family, but he expected they would pressure him to settle and farm in the area as they had done before. For all he knew, his parents were no longer living. He considered hunting and trapping along the Missouri closer to Saint Louis, but why do that when greater opportunities were further up the Missouri River in Montana. Colter knew that he would collect $178 upon his return to Saint Louis, so he pondered how he might spend these funds. One idea was to collect his money and fund a trapping trip back up the Missouri. The supplies for such a trip would include powder, lead, traps, sewing supplies, more knives and various food supplies plus a boat for the long journey. He also considered the need for trading goods to gain favor with the Indians he would likely encounter. Colter lived his life as a subsistence hunter with little capital or financial standing to do anything but subsist by hunting and trapping then selling what was needed to purchase or barter for goods he could not produce himself. His hunting and trapping skills had served him well, so he wondered where those skills would serve him best. At age thirty-one, Colter was in good health and did not consider any physical limitations to continuing to live as he always had.

After Ordway's group of river canoeists joined Lewis on the Missouri River, Colter's hunting skills were once again challenged to provide for a large group of hungry men. Colter and a companion walked away from the river hunting for buffalo, deer and elk and killed six buffalo, thirteen deer, five elk and thirty-one beaver. During their hunt, they miscalculated their position relative to Lewis and the main body, thinking that they were ahead of Lewis. Due to this miscalculation, Collins and Colter waited for Lewis then determined their mistake and started their journey down the river to catch Lewis and the main body. After nine days absent, Colter and Collins caught Lewis who had halted his group to engage two whites who were camped along the Missouri River. These two men had left Saint Louis two years prior in hopes of harvesting the gains from the lucrative beaver trade. The two men told Lewis they were from the Illinois country possessing twenty good traps and had had good fortune trapping along the Missouri and caching some of their pelts. Their good fortune had ended with an encounter with the Lakota Teton who took most of their pelts and some of their gear. In the confrontation, one of the men was injured and they both felt fortunate to have escaped up the river. Lewis took some of their precious time to inform the two trappers of the challenges that lay ahead. One of the trappers grew more concerned as he listened to Lewis and announced that they would return to the Mandan village to find a Frenchman or someone to guide them up the Missouri. Seeing their desperate situation, Lewis gave the two men a file, powder and some lead. Lewis was about to take leave of the two from Illinois country when Colter and his companion paddled onto the riverbank and joined this chance encounter on the Missouri. As Colter climbed out of his canoe he heard a familiar voice exclaim, "well, I'll be damned if that is not John Colter!" Standing on the river bank was Forrest Hancock.

CHAPTER FIVE
Beaver Fever

Nikolai Petrovich Rezanov was an ambitious man. As he sailed past the mast of the *Amherst* still visible above the waves, Rezanov considered the opportunity that might lie to the east where the great Columbia River emptied into the Pacific. The American captain of Rezanov's ship warned of the lurking sandbars lying just below the surface where the Columbia River collided with the Pacific. The Russians did not have access to the navigation charts developed by the British and Americans, so they ignored Columbia's siren song. There were eight Boston-based ships plying the Pacific waters and several of these ships were part of the Russian-American Company (RAC) and the growing fur trade. The sea otter and fur seal furs were bringing record prices in the Orient and Rezanov wanted to expand production to further enrich his family's assets and those of the RAC. The otter population in Alaska was in decline and the RAC knew of more abundant otter populations further south along the American coast. In addition, the Alaskan outposts were not adequately provisioned, so the RAC needed a food supply from the Spanish outposts in California or possibly a new Russian outpost in a more hospitable environment. As Rezanov sailed along the Oregon coast little did he know that just miles to the east rested men who would become competitors in the world trade of furs.

Out of necessity, the Russians depended on animal furs to survive the brutal Russian winters. More recently, there had emerged new hat styles that symbolized a gentleman's status whether he be civilian or military. The vast majority of these hats were made from the wool of the beaver. The Russians were innovators in developing new technologies for processing beaver pelts. A beaver pelt consists of skin and guard hairs with a layer of "wool" between these two layers. Removing beaver guard hair made felting with the beaver wool more efficient by "combing" out the unwanted hairs and producing a high-quality wool for felting hats. Felt is stronger than woven materials, and is resistant to water and beaver wool was ideal for felting. The rising popularity of felted hats in Western Europe pushed up the demand for beaver wool and Russia was the prime source of beaver wool for French, Spanish and British hat makers. When the French, Spanish and British started bringing beaver pelts from America, a new class of beaver pelt emerged. Due to the importance of separating the beaver wool from the guard hairs, the Europeans would pay premium prices for beaver garments (coat beaver) worn by Indians and whites. When the pelts had been worn for a year, the guard hairs would release, leaving the wool exposed and more accessible for making garments.

After the French defeat at the hands of the British and American colonists in the Seven Years War, the British gained control of the fur trade in most of North America. The Hudson Bay Company (HBC) had received a royal charter in 1670 and in 1763 it had the opportunity to control the fur trade and control it they did. While the French strategy had been to penetrate deep into the North American frontier and live with the Indians, the British strategy had been to build trading posts and forts and invite the Indians to trade with them. The HBC developed a market for furs in a barter system that valued beaver pelts relative to the goods brought from Britain. The Indians sought cloth goods, tobacco, beads, kettles, knives, needles, flints, gunpowder, guns and other iron goods in exchange for the furs and pelts they owned. The HBC would barter with the Indians then ship the pelts to Europe where they would be sold for hard currency. The basis of the barter trade with the Indians was a "made beaver" pelt, which required the pelt to meet minimum standards with regard to scraping and drying the pelt, but was not a "coat beaver" with the guard hairs removed. One "made beaver" could buy a powder horn or ice chisel, while fourteen "made beaver" would pay for a gun. The HBC would then ship the beaver pelts to London, where it would sell the pelt for $1.20 to $1.80(actually sold in British shillings) per pelt depending on the year and the market price.

The French had moved up the Mississippi and down the Saint Lawrence to settle and intermarry with the Indians while the British started to the north in Hudson Bay and moved south and west into the Canadian hinterland. The French married Indian women while the British signed treaties with tribal chiefs and sought commercial advantages. The British, unlike the restless American settlers to the south, had no desire to settle territory. The British Crown and the HBC had mercantile interests to satisfy, so upsetting the Indians by challenging them for control over land was not in their plans. The British were very adept at cultivating strong relationships with selected, powerful tribes like the Shawnee, the Iroquois Confederacy, the Cree and the Iron Confederacy. The Iron Confederacy of the central Canadian Plains was a powerful political and economic force greatly due to its relationship with the British. They operated as middle men between the Plains Indians and the HBC and as such they procured the guns, powder and lead needed to establish political power on the Plains. The Blackfeet tribe was a predominant trading partner with the Iron Confederacy, trading their horses, buffalo skin, robes and furs for European goods, including guns and ammunition. This relationship based on economic, linguistic and geopolitical factors made both the Cree and the Blackfeet powerful tribes in their respective lands. The flow of British goods down from the Hudson Bay established these tribes as powerful and wealthy peoples compared to most of the Plains tribes to their south. While the Teton Sioux were a force on the Missouri River, the Blackfeet would prove to be a far more powerful force in the plentiful beaver rivers at the foot of the Rocky Mountains.

The five divided groups of the Corps of Discovery were now one, gathering at the Mandan village that had treated them so well during their winter quarters in 1804-1805. The men were eager to continue their swift decent down the Missouri, knowing that the current that had bedeviled them in 1804 was now their friend heading toward Saint Louis. With so many stories and artifacts in their possession it was no wonder they were eager to return to Saint Louis and their families beyond. While Sacagawea and her baby boy and the boy's father, Toussaint Charbonneau, would remain with the Mandan, the rest of the party would continue downstream to be reunited with family and friends. The two men who had met the Corps were not of the same mindset. They left friends and family behind in Illinois and Missouri to find wealth in the beaver rivers and ponds that lay to the west. Dixon and Hancock were not motivated by the adventure of discovery and the unknown. They were "gold seekers" looking for wealth they had not found in farming and hunting in Illinois and Missouri. What they heard from Lewis shook their confidence and changed their calculation of risk and reward. First, the prime beaver trapping was much farther away than they had expected. Second, the threats from Indians and bears raised considerable concern about their personal safety. Third, they had already lost most of their supplies and many of their furs to hostile Indians. Dixon and Hancock were seriously considering turning back unless they could find an experienced and knowledgeable guide to join them. Hancock was thrilled to see Colter.

Hancock had left Kentucky with the Boones, looking for better hunting grounds than those remaining in Kentucky. The farmers and settlers were controlling Kentucky and the supply of wild game was diminishing just as it had in Virginia and the East as settlements grew. Living along the Missouri River, Hancock heard many stories of the abundant beaver grounds to the west and the prices of beaver pelts in Saint Louis could make him a rich man. Unlike the British, the Americans would trap their own beaver and sell the pelts themselves to the French traders in Saint Louis and New Orleans. Like Colter, Hancock had no strong attachment to family and was not married. At age thirty, there were few women on the frontier who would be interested in Hancock due to his prospects and age. Going west and striking it rich with beaver pelts made sense to him. Now his old friend Colter "dropped out of the sky" and his mind started to calculate: what would it take to entice John Colter to join him and Dixon in their pursuit of beaver riches?

Hancock, being a veteran of the Shawnee battles, found a friend in Clark. Hancock approached Clark with the idea of giving Colter an early discharge from the Corps to serve the purpose of exploring and exploiting the riches that lay to the west. Clark was very supportive of the idea if Colter was given the opportunity to explore some of the rivers feeding the Yellowstone and the Missouri that the Corps had not fully explored. Hancock agreed to Clark's terms so Clark in turn approached Lewis with the idea of sending a Corps member back into some of the country they had not fully explored and establishing commercial relations with Indians whom Jefferson wanted to engage in commerce. Colter's mind was set on moving down the Missouri like the rest of the Corps, what would he think of this proposal? Colter had not seen his mother, father and siblings in three years. Were they still living? Would he be received well as a hunter and explorer? What were his prospects in Kentucky?

With Clark's blessings, Hancock and Dixon devised a plan. They would offer Colter shares in their endeavor, which included supplies and twenty beaver traps they had managed to keep and the pelts they would take to Saint Louis. In addition, Colter would have an opportunity to explore rivers feeding the Yellowstone and the Missouri that had not been explored by the Corps. With the Corps ready to move downstream, Hancock approached Colter with his proposal. Colter balked at the idea of abandoning the Corps of men he served. He had lingering thoughts of inadequacy based on recent events, but still his loyalty to the Corps of Discovery was strong. Colter approached Clark with the idea, expecting Clark to reject the proposal. To Colter's surprise, Clark encouraged Colter to join Hancock and Dixon with the goal of both exploring some rivers and exploiting the beaver trade. With Clark's support, Colter began to contemplate returning to the rolling landscapes, cascading rivers and plentiful valleys that had so thrilled him.

On a warm August night, Colter stood next to the river that had carried him to lands spectacular and filled with wildlife. One more time he considered his prospects in Saint Louis or back in Kentucky. He also considered Clark's desire for further exploration of the rivers feeding the Missouri and the Yellowstone. The business proposal from Hancock and Dixon was a factor, but not a compelling one. Colter's life focused on survival in the wilds, and accumulating wealth never appealed to him. Other members of the Corps would write their own accounts of the great adventure into the Northwest, but Colter was more interested in more adventure and expanding the unknown frontier of Clark's new America. The most compelling factor to Colter was Clark's desire for further exploration of the rivers feeding the Yellowstone and the Missouri. Clark thought highly of Colter and Colter sensed this admiration, which touched him deeply. Here among many resourceful and brave men, Colter had earned the admiration of Clark. Colter decided that he would tell Clark of his willingness to further explore the rivers that Clark so desired to put on his map.

When Colter informed Clark of his decision, Clark was overjoyed, but there was one provision. Lewis would not permit Colter an early discharge if it would lead to more men seeking a similar discharge from the Corp of Discovery. Clark and Lewis decided that before allowing Colter an early discharge, the men of the Corps must understand that this was a singular exception and that all the remaining men must complete their enlistment until Saint Louis. Clark told Colter that each man of the Corps would be asked to commit to stay with the Corps until Saint Louis if they agreed to give Colter his early discharge. Colter doubted that he would get favorable treatment. In his mind, the return journey had not gone well and his status in the Corps suffered from several embarrassments and confrontations. He thought he would get some support, but getting the entire Corps to agree to special dispensation was a long shot. Having spent much of the journey hunting and isolated from the main group, Colter did not develop relationships with most of the men and among the few he had spent time he doubted their assessment of him.

Clark polled the men and each man of the Corps agreed to remain with the expedition to Saint Louis. The polling of the men revealed a common admiration of Colter. Their agreement to remain with the Corps was a gesture of respect to one who had performed his duty so well and each man wished Colter every success. At this moment, Colter realized that his many solitary efforts to feed the Corps and quietly support their common good had not gone unnoticed. Lewis and Clark added to Colter's sense of satisfaction by generously giving him powder, lead and his prized rifle that Lewis had procured at Harper's Ferry. As "the man in the corner" and "the unseen man of the expedition," these gestures gave Colter a quiet satisfaction and a memory that would remain with him the rest of his life.

On a cool August Saturday morning, Colter climbed into the canoe looking up at the faces of the Corps of Discovery. Not being a sentimental man, Colter felt little sadness departing from the Corps with whom he had been almost three years, experiencing many trials and adventures. Clark stood stoically at the river's edge watching one of his most trusted "soldiers" turn his canoe into the current and as Colter did so Clark saluted the man he hoped to see again.

The three trappers had enough provisions for a two-year trip into the Rockies plus the twenty beaver traps they hoped would make their travels a financial success. After discussions with Lewis, Clark and Ordway, the three decided they would move off the Missouri and take the Yellowstone River into the Rockies. This was the route taken by Clark and his detachment on the return trip, while Colter and the remainder of the Corps traveled east on more northerly routes. All three were very aware of the Lewis encounter with the Blackfeet, and the Crow Indians told the Corps of the Blackfeet threat to anyone entering their claimed territory. Clark reported seeing many beavers along the Yellowstone and its tributaries, so avoiding the Blackfeet and trapping in rivers full of beaver was logical. In addition, Colter wanted to honor Clark's request for more information about the headwaters of the Big Horn and Yellowstone rivers.

As the three paddled up the Missouri there were numerous disputes about where and how often to stop. Choosing a camping spot was particularly contentious and one day the dispute went on so long that it was near nightfall when Colter steered the canoe to the shore. Colter was the most experienced canoeist and hunter, so he usually was in the stern and did the hunting while Dixon and Hancock did camp chores. This caused Dixon to complain ad nauseam about the arrangement. Adding to Dixon's discontent were the many experiences shared by Colter and Hancock in Kentucky and the sharing of memories and stories of those years. When the three travelers turned their canoe into the Yellowstone River there was a noticeable change in current, as the Yellowstone flowed much faster than the Missouri, making paddling more difficult with a canoe filled with 130 pounds of steel traps and chains plus other supplies. Dixon seldom paddled his share, claiming his injury at the hands of the Teton was limiting his strength.

Even with the Yellowstone slowing their progress, the three would be at the foot of the Rockies in time to trap in the fall season when the beaver coats were thickest and most desirable. For many days, the Rockies rose in the west as the Yellowstone plunged south and west flowing between high plateaus and among cottonwoods, willows, pines and high brush. As the paddlers pushed up stream, the first signs of fall appeared in the golds and yellows in the trees and brush. On several occasions the men would navigate a sharp bend in the river only to confront a grizzly bear "fishing" for the day's catch. Surprising a grizzly bear resulted in the men trying to confuse the bear with noise and waving paddles, but on two occasions guns were required to shoot the charging bear. Stopping a charging grizzly with lead from a musket or rifle took a particular skill. The immense size and dense fur of the bear required a head or neck shot and sometimes two shots. Colter's .54 caliber rifle lead brought down bear's huge chest and Dixon missed the huge target altogether.

As the men approached the Rockies the prevalence of beaver was impressive. Clark's accounts were no exaggeration. Deciding where to camp for a night was easy compared to choosing where to set up camp for the trapping season. Colter had limited expertise in the art of beaver trapping. He had performed his duty of getting the small party to the Rockies, now Dixon and Hancock would apply their skills. There were several considerations in setting up camp, including the prevalence of beaver, the exposure to indigenous tribes and bears, protection from wind, and availability of game and wood. After three days of searching, Dixon and Hancock agreed on a location near a large collection of streams and ponds surrounded by willow and cottonwood. The "forest" of willow and cottonwood stumps indicated a large active beaver population. The camp was struck on an island in the Clarks Fork River, which provided some protection from Indians and bears. The dense brush and trees lining the rivers limited visibility of approaching Indians or marauding bears.

Beaver trapping was wet, arduous work. Beaver traps were set four to six inches under the surface of the stream or the surface of the pond. The trap was then anchored in the deeper water with a long pole fashioned from a dead cottonwood branch that was attached to the chain running to the trap. The beaver was attracted to the trap with a stick covered with the fluid from the beaver's castoreum glands. Once set, the trap would be checked one to two times per day. Setting twenty traps required finding multiple ponds and streams and walking between these locations each day. The hardest work in beaver trapping was bringing the heavy beavers back to camp where they would be skinned with sharpened knives, scraping the fat and meat from the skin then stretching and drying the pelt. As the three men began setting traps, Colter's trained eyes found grizzly scat and tracks then later the same day tracks left by twelve ponies. Colter advised Dixon and Hancock that their location was not the best, but the two ambitious trappers clearly had "beaver fever." It took five days to set all twenty traps across an area several miles wide and long on either side of the Clarks Fork. Colter advised that the three men travel together always when checking traps for defensive purposes. This plan proved to be important when the third day they surprised a four-hundred-pound grizzly sow eating berries near one of the ponds where they had traps. The first week of trapping produced one hundred ninety large pelts worth four hundred dollars. After having lost most of their pelts to the Teton and enduring the difficulties of the two-thousand-mile journey, Dixon and Hancock were being rewarded and their beaver fever was reaching new highs.

Colter had trapped, hunted and skinned animals most of his life. He did not share the beaver fever that enveloped his companions. Dixon's continuous complaining, the soggy and routine business of checking traps and drying skins, the careless nature of both Dixon and Hancock and the clouds of mosquitos were all weighing down Colter's desire for a two-year enterprise with his partners. By mid-October Colter was ready to move out. He informed his partners that he would be travelling light and would not be taking pelts or traps with him. As a partner, he expected to be paid his share for the pelts they had trapped and dried, but he doubted he would ever see the money. Money was needed for powder, lead, flint, files and salt. Colter was eager to find the headwaters of the Yellowstone and the Big Horn Rivers. Colter was driven by Clark's curiosity and his own desire to satisfy his captain's goal of creating a map of the new Louisiana Territory. With his thirty-pound pack and trusted rifle, Colter left camp and headed west.

CHAPTER SIX
Seeking the River's Headwaters

Finding the headwaters of the Yellowstone would require walking along the Clarks Fork, as it twisted into the west. Clark had told Colter that the Yellowstone first flowed north when he had joined it on his return journey, so Colter expected to find the Yellowstone somewhere to his west. There was one problem with this plan: the Beartooth Mountains.

Traveling alone was not foreign to Colter as he had hunted for the Corps as a solitary hunter. He was also accustomed to traveling into lands totally foreign to him with destination unknown. During his many solitary travels, Colter developed his senses to a point never experienced by most humans. Survival sharpens the senses like nothing else. His hearing was developed to the point that Dixon's chatter was upsetting to him. Night listening was particularly acute, as Colter was attuned to a branch breaking, a dried leaf being crushed, breathing sounds, the cessation of insects buzzing or frogs croaking or the sound of feet moving in the river. Colter's eyes were programmed to watch for scat, tracks, broken branches, dead animals, flattened grass, unusual movement of nearby buffalo or wild horses, and rising smoke or dust on the horizon. While Colter's senses were first attuned to threats, they were also attuned to the hunt. Sometimes the need for food compromised his desire for concealment as firing his rifle announced his position. There were nights that Colter could not sleep given his overly keen senses and at times imagined threats.

The second day into his journey, the river entered a deep, narrow gorge forcing Colter to climb back into the valley below and look for another path through the mountains. He picked up an Indian trail and fresh elk tracks that might lead him to a meal of fresh meat that night and an opportunity to dry meat for his trip into the high country where game would be sparse. The golden grasses surrounding him waved in stark contrast to the red rock outcroppings that interrupted the landscape of grasses and pines. After climbing three thousand feet, he reached the top of the pass and was stopped by the vista unfolding before his eyes. A lush valley lay below with golden deciduous trees; the Beartooth Mountains lay to the north and the Absaroka mountains lay to the west and south with their high peaks covered in snow. The Bitterroot Mountains had presented great beauty, but at this point in his life, Colter had never seen such a sight. The Absaroka spires sat above the lush valley as if keeping watch. As he sat and considered his path forward, he felt that in a way this valley somehow belonged to him, or was it the reverse? Colter's sense of belonging to the wilds was heightened by the provision of food and beauty given to him by the land. Not wanting to leave this spot, Colter decided to camp there and enjoy his dried meat and berries. The sunset was soon followed by a full moon rising and illuminating the snow-capped Absaroka across the valley.

After packing his buffalo robe and supplies, Colter began his descent through the pines and grasses as he followed a dry creek. He was seeing plenty of grizzly markers, but no signs of Indians. He doubted there would be Indians in the high meadows and valleys this late in the year. The distant peaks were now a day's trip in his front. As he entered the valley floor, he found a deep gorge with a stream running through it that he followed until the gorge flattened out providing good access to the reduced fall water flow. Finding a good camping spot, Colter enjoyed a loin cut from the elk he had shot the day before. That night he slept surprisingly well until being awakened in the dawn light by a sound coming from the creek. The sound was much like two rocks being struck together. Colter grabbed his rifle and loaded then crept down to the creek. There standing among the rocks lining the creek was a chestnut stallion looking as startled as Colter. The two creatures stared at each other for several minutes, each now realizing that they shared this place with another. Wild horses seldom separate from their herd. How had this stallion become isolated? Was he imprisoned by the steep valley walls or had he become separated from the herd then decided to remain in this grass-rich highland. Was he driven out of the herd by a younger stallion? Horses remained in their herd for protection, so being isolated put a solitary horse at risk, especially in an area inhabited by mighty grizzlies. Colter considered approaching the stallion, but he would get no closer as the chestnut turned away into the pines.

Colter continued following the stream until it completely disappeared. After two days of walking west toward the mountain peaks, Colter spotted a "saddle" in the mountains and started toward that point. He was confident that the headwaters of the Yellowstone were still ahead of him. Colter determined his best route over the mountain and started climbing two thousand feet to his chosen mountain pass. Arriving at his mountain pass, Colter saw below him another golden valley dotted with ponds and divided by another mountain stream running to the west. After his long climb up the mountain, Colter was ready for a good night's sleep under his buffalo robe. In the morning, he awoke to a dusting of snow that covered his robe and his entire surroundings, making him a part of this wonderland. As he descended into the valley, he picked up the trail of several large elk he hoped to overtake for his evening meal. Halfway down the mountain he spotted a large elk browsing on some tree branches oblivious to the presence of one of history's great hunters. It took only one shot at one hundred yards and Colter's desire for fresh meat was satisfied. As Colter dressed out his elk he heard branches snapping behind him and turned to see a six-hundred-pound grizzly boar charging from the trees. Knowing he had not enough time to load his rifle, Colter grabbed his gear and scrambled down the mountain expecting the bear to claim his elk rather than chase Colter down the mountain. As expected and hoped, the bear stopped near the half-dressed elk and circled as if to gloat over his easily won prize. It was Colter's good fortune that the slight breeze blowing down the mountain side kept his presence unknown to the boar as he feasted on the elk carcass. At one hundred ten yards, Colter had a clear shot at the boar and he thought his one available shot had found its mark in the bear's head. However, the bear came roaring down the mountain and Colter remembered Lewis's requirement that all hunters be in pairs to ensure a second shot at a charging grizzly. Colter's next most lethal weapon was his tomahawk, which he threw with great accuracy. Colter stood his ground as he watched a monster cover the one hundred ten yards to within the ten yards needed for a fatal tomahawk throw. Colter's strength multiplied as his adrenaline peaked and his tomahawk was thrown with such force it laid open the bear's brains. With the bear lying at his feet and his heart racing, Colter smiled and wiped the bear's blood from his face.

Colter now had a choice between fresh bear meat and fresh elk meat. Since he had already started dressing the elk, he proceeded to take the loin and hind meat from the elk. Roasting the loin would provide a fine meal that night and the hind meat would dry nicely. The trip down into the basin was an easy trip covering three thousand vertical feet in no time at all. Colter moved south following the north-flowing river he thought to be the Yellowstone. Soon Colter was walking above a deep gorge formed by the river and its turbulent rush to the north. As the sun was getting low, Colter came upon a most beautiful sight. Before him was a deep blue lake framed by high mountain peaks to the south and rimmed with golden aspen. The next morning Colter enjoyed the last of his fresh elk meat and walked through the aspens at lake's edge until he came to a southeast arm of the lake where the river continued southeast into the mountains to the east.

It had been months since he had seen the Big Horn River. Clark believed that, like the Yellowstone River, the Big Horn's headwaters existed in these magnificent mountains. The high peaks to the west formed a barrier to the Yellowstone and most certainly the Big Horn as well. While the Yellowstone flowed north, the Big Horn must lie to the south given the fact that the Big Horn flowed into the Yellowstone from the south. Heading south and east, Colter followed a river that snaked through a grass-covered valley. As Colter moved through the valley he was impressed if not intimidated by the height of the peaks ahead of him. These peaks were higher and more formidable than those he had climbed on his way to the great mountain lake. Colter kept following the river as it grew smaller, winding around the base of a huge snow-covered peak. The river, now a stream, went around to the back side of the mountain where it abruptly ended at the base of a snow field.

It had been weeks since he had seen a human and several days since he had seen any elk or deer. He had seen tracks from a wolf pack that made him nervous and could explain the lack of deer and elk. Colter had adequate supplies of dried meat and a bag full of pine nuts and he had been fortunate to walk into a meadow full of miner's lettuce along the mountain stream he had been following.

With no river to follow, Colter headed east following an animal trail down the contour of the mountain. After crossing a snow field, he once again found a stream hurrying down the mountain side. Several hours down the stream Colter found a hospitable valley that cut away to the south dodging more high peaks. Unfortunately, the valley narrowed and became impassable forcing Colter to climb up the mountainside to the east. His progress was greatly slowed as night approached, so he perched on a rocky mountainside burying himself under his buffalo robe. During the night, a heavy snowfall started to bury Colter, which forced him to stand, shake off the snow that had accumulated on him and create a burrow in the deepening snow. The next day was very slow going in the deep early fall snow. It was now imperative that Colter descend as fast as possible with heavier snows approaching at higher elevations. Moving down the mountainside among trees became easier as the snow depth lessened and the slope of the mountain provided direction to the lower elevations he sought. Stumbling out of the forest he walked onto a flatter, rocky plain that offered another stream to follow as it journeyed toward the east. The scene below was startling in contrasts as the light snow rested upon ridges and foothills decorated with red stone.

Some miles away, Colter could see the unmistakable smoke from an Indian village. With winter approaching this offered Colter a good opportunity for shelter and resupply for the spring trip ahead. The question to be answered was "which Indian peoples resided in this village?" Colter moved closer to the village as night fell. There would be no camp fire tonight. In the morning, Colter found a high spot to observe the Indians to determine their tribal identity. At midmorning, two young men rode out of the village on their horses headed toward Colter. As they approached, Colter clearly saw their long flowing hair as they rode, an unmistakable trait of a male Crow Indian. Colter stepped out from his hiding spot and greeted the two young men in their native language. He had learned a few Crow words from Sacagawea that he used to express his friendly intentions and used sign language to ask for their hospitality. Sacagawea knew the Crow to be a friendly people as they were friendly to the Hidatsa, Mandan, Shoshone and Nez Perce with whom they shared common enemies. The Crow tribe was looking for strong allies as the Blackfeet and the Teton were pushing them off prime buffalo hunting lands. They were excellent horsemen and horse thieves, but had relatively few guns compared to the Blackfeet and Teton. While the Crow welcomed the Americans as a potential ally, there was another factor in Colter's request for hospitality. A solitary man coming in peace received a warm welcome and with the coming of winter the Crow understood their obligation and opportunity to treat this stranger with great hospitality.

The two young men were members of the Fox society, one of three warrior societies in the village, and they eagerly led Colter into the village to be formally greeted by their chief. As Colter walked through the encampment of eighty teepees he was most impressed with the colorful artistry on the teepees. There were many children in the village who had never seen anyone like Colter. Two young boys dared each other to touch him as if to count coups, but neither dared to come close to the man with hair on his face carrying a rifle and a long knife and tomahawk hanging from his waist. While the men wore their hair very long, many of the women had cut their hair. Colter recognized that these women were in mourning for the death of a loved one. Word traveled fast to the Fox Society Chief and he was waiting for Colter beside his teepee. The chief's name was White Dog and he was the proud father of two sons and a daughter. He invited Colter into the teepee and issued an invitation to share his teepee with Colter. This invitation was willingly accepted. That night the chief hosted a feast attended by the Fox Society members. Colter was honored with buffalo tongue as the others ate other buffalo cuts. The evening continued with the hot dance around the large fire followed by several young men telling of their bravery during the recent battle with the Blackfeet. Colter did not understand all accounts of the battle, but it was apparent that the Blackfeet had numerous guns while the Crow relied on spears and arrows. The Crow prevailed in the battle, but at great cost. The fourteen scalps hanging from the dance poles brought honor to the Fox Society and some relief from the grief carried by the many women encircling and dancing as they told the story of the battle.

Colter's winter with the Crow taught him a good deal about their customs, their economy, their relationships, their spirituality and their good nature. Colter brought ample game to White Dog's teepee and enjoyed telling of the America he knew. White Dog's wife provided Colter with five new pairs of moccasins and a new buckskin shirt. He helped the family skin deer then dry the skins and smoke the meat. By March, Colter was well provisioned and eager to continue his search for the headwaters of the Big Horn River. The night before his departure the entire village gathered for feast, dancing and more storytelling. White Dog honored Colter with a chicken hawk feather to be worn on his head as White Dog had a dream of Colter traveling over many rivers and mountains as a bird. At daybreak, the next morning White Dog was waiting for Colter as he emerged from the teepee with his final gift. White Dog was holding the reins of a fine-looking mare taken from his hard-won herd of thirty horses. Colter was greatly honored because he understood that a Crow's wealth and status was related to the number of horses he owned. In addition, two Crow men would accompany him to the Yellowstone River.

Colter's winter with the Crow proved to be very helpful in finding the headwaters of the Big Horn River. The Crow informed him that the river flowing out of the mountains to the south suddenly turned to the north and flowed into the Yellowstone where Colter expected the Big Horn to join the Yellowstone. Confident he had found the headwaters of the Big Horn, Colter and his companions turned north. Colter wanted to find the river that would take him back to the Yellowstone and then the Missouri River. Riding on horseback, Colter could more than double his miles in a day, but even more important was a sense that he had recovered dominion over his environs. Living among the Crow with their comforts and now riding atop a fine horse delivered him from the existence known only to a man walking in hostile terrain not knowing where the valley ended nor how long his food supply would last. Colter's horse gave him the luxury of searching for gentler passes and flatter plateaus as he probed the hills and mountains standing between him and the river that would take him to Saint Louis.

Taking an Indian trail north, the three men climbed up to a high plateau that afforded them a view of distant mountains familiar to Colter, for these were the mountains that created the basin where he knew he would find the Clarks Fork. Riding along the eastern base of high mountains, the game was plentiful and the terrain friendly to his journey. The trip north became somewhat predicable and even boring given Colter's history of journeying through the unknown and unpredictable. This all changed late one afternoon as Colter approached a valley with numerous rising plumes of what appeared to be smoke. His first thought was an Indian village, but the two Crow tried to explain that the earth was providing this mysterious display of "clouds." Drawing closer and making observations convinced Colter that this was not a village, as there was no sign of human activity nor habitation. As Colter rode closer, the land became stranger than anything he had ever seen. The "smoke" was not just smoke but steam and smoke billowing from the earth in great eruptions as if the earth was disgorging itself of unwanted matter. The sound was equally mysterious as the earth burped and bellowed through gaps and caverns in the ground. The most memorable feature of the place, to be known as "Colter's Hell," was the stench of sulfuric odors that burned the nostrils. The land was so toxic that neither grass nor tree would grow. The two Crow warned Colter that no man should venture among the "earth clouds" as the earth was likely to consume any such foolish man. As Colter's horse wandered into the fields of fires, the horse began to stumble as the ground gave way and threatened to swallow both man and horse. Terrified by the prospect, Colter reined his horse to the nearest point free of the steam and smoke and onto solid ground.

Continuing north, Colter finally reached the Clarks Fork and found the trapper's camp where he had last seen Dixon and Hancock some five hundred miles and seven months ago. The remnants of the camp were there, but no sign of the two men. Colter had no need of these two men. He had found the headwaters of the rivers that Clark desired to know. He carried no beaver pelts, but did carry a vast knowledge of the mountains and rivers that no person of European descent possessed. His respect for the indigenous peoples had grown over his journey; once again reaffirming the fact that they knew a great deal about these lands and that newcomers like himself would need their support. Colter rode his Crow horse up to the point where the river widened and there was a good stand of cottonwood trees from which to fashion his canoe. It took the better part of a morning to chop through a big cottonwood with his axe and begin the process of digging and burning out his sitting place in the trunk of the tree that would carry him eleven hundred miles down the Yellowstone and Missouri rivers. With the help of his two traveling companions, the canoe was ready for the long trip in two days. Early one morning, Colter rose and stood before his two new friends and thanked them for their company and returned the chief's mare for their trip to the Crow village. As Colter pushed off into the river, he turned to see the two mounted men caught in the rising sun and signaling their farewell.

CHAPTER SEVEN
Dying for Business

Manual Lisa lived on the edge of Saint Louis society. He was a Spaniard who for some brief months wielded power emanating from the Spanish crown, only to be undermined by the French then American powers. Few who ever did business with him liked him or trusted him, but his relentless and fearless pursuit of riches from the fur trade garnered some respect from the Saint Louis establishment. Lisa was among the first to see economic opportunity in the new frontier, much like the gold miners who would follow years later. The riches of the Louisiana Territory drew Lisa north from New Orleans only to find that Frenchmen and the now newly arrived Americans stood in his way. Lisa was well acquainted with the ships taking American beaver pelts to Europe and the high prices being paid for these pelts. His early attempts at securing pelts from the tribes nearer to Saint Louis had been blocked by the Chouteau family, so his ambition now pushed him up the Missouri River to the lands open to newcomers like himself. Even before Lewis and Clark returned to Saint Louis, Lisa prepared to exploit the beaver-rich lands of the Louisiana Territory. When the Corps of Discovery returned to Saint Louis, Lisa pounced on the accumulated knowledge and experience by hiring eight members of the Corps to serve his efforts on the upper Missouri. With his Saint Louis partners, William Morrison and Pierre Menard, Lisa was eager to exploit the opportunity.

Lisa fashioned a new approach to exploiting the beaver-rich lands up the Missouri. Rather than relying on Indian villages to trap and supply him with beaver pelts, he would supplement the Indian pelt supplies with pelts produced by his own men whom he would send into the rivers and ponds rich with beaver. He knew the Plains Indians lived off the buffalo and they had developed the skills of hunting and processing buffalo. The taking of beaver and processing their skins was a sidelight for most of the Plains Indians. The British enticed the Indians to supply them with beaver pelts by trading European goods for pelts. Lisa understood this to be a limiting factor to his great ambition. He intended to build a series of "forts" to trade with the Indians and as points from which to send his men on beaver trapping missions.

The spring following the return of the Corps to Saint Louis, Lisa gathered sixty men and an armada of keel boats for the twenty-six-hundred-mile trip up the Missouri River. Each was loaded with the necessities of survival plus the goods needed to trade with the Indians. As Lisa's men struggled against the Missouri's current, paddling, poling and pulling the boats, they passed numerous tributaries and tribes controlled by the powerful Chouteau family. Knowing that these tribes would have little to do with him, the Lisa expedition moved on up the river. As Lisa's expedition left the territory controlled by the Chouteau family at the Platte River, who should appear but John Colter. Colter was a solitary figure moving down the Missouri at great pace with little in his canoe beyond his vast knowledge of prime beaver trapping grounds and the Indians who inhabited these grounds. Lisa could not believe his luck as Colter knew more about the rivers and mountains at the headwaters of the Missouri than any man of European descent. Lisa immediately made Colter an offer that included a wage, a portion of the profits from the expedition and an opportunity to lead men into the lands he had grown to love.

Not having found Dickson and Hancock, Colter proceeded down the Yellowstone and the Missouri rivers taking advantage of the strong current to reach the Platte River on June 28, 1807. Colter's plan was to return to Saint Louis and convey his discoveries to Clark. Having spent more than a month in his solitary journey past both hostile and friendly Indian villages, Colter was already missing the life he had been living. What he missed was more than the stark beauty of the lands he had discovered. He missed the intoxicating edge of survival, the encounter with every sound, the dogged search for enemy and game. Lisa's offer was reminiscent of the proposition made by Dixon and Hancock; finances were of little interest to Colter compared to the roulette of surviving in the headwaters of the Missouri. Lisa offered Colter a unique position in his company of men. Colter would not be required to sign the three-year contract that each member had signed and he would be free to move and trap on his account once the company arrived at its destination. He was also offered a salary for his time if he would lead the company to the territory he knew. Colter was no longer one among equals, but now held a position of esteem derived from his experiences and exploits in the mountains and valleys that lay ahead of Lisa's company. The success of Lisa's company now greatly depended upon Colter's knowledge and leadership.

Colter's survival in solitude was now abruptly and noisily interrupted. He now traveled with a group of loud, unruly men working for Lisa, who were seeking wealth and adventure. Colter had had his own experience with adventure and experienced it in silence with an urgency grounded in sustenance and protection from the elements and predators. This collection of humanity could not compare to the intimate encounter he endured in his journey into the mountains and down into the valleys. If Colter or any one of Lisa's hunters failed to bring in fresh meat, another hunter would succeed. As a solitary traveler, Colter's existence depended on his own success. After several encounters with hunger, Colter came to realize that it was not his success that provided for his needs, but the generosity of the lands he traveled that sustained him.

It soon became apparent to Colter that Lisa's company was not the Corps of Discovery. Unlike Lewis or Clark, Lisa was unpredictable and tempestuous. There was no stopping to collect specimens nor establish latitude and longitude. Lisa was pushing to get his men up the river to build the first fort before the winter started. Lisa's company was already behind schedule and would miss the fall trapping season. There had been much discontent among the men and one had disserted only to be tracked down and shot rather than court-martialed, as would have been done on a military expedition such as the Corps of Discovery. Much to Colter's discontent, George Drouillard was one of the Corps' members in Lisa's employ, but much to his delight it was now Colter who held the special position apart from the other men. Lisa consulted with

Colter regarding the destination and optimal location of their first fort. Colter counseled Lisa that the Yellowstone was full of beaver and the Indians populating the Yellowstone Valley were much friendlier. Given his newfound knowledge of the Yellowstone and the Big Horn rivers, Colter counseled Lisa to build his fort at the juncture of the Yellowstone and the Big Horn rivers.

It was November 1807 when Lisa's company reached the juncture of the Yellowstone and the Big Horn rivers. The men quickly set to building their stockade, including two large buildings to house Lisa and his key men plus the trading goods and the other to house the rest of the men. It was an ideal spot where the game was plentiful, there was wood for construction and coal for heating and cooking and the friendly Crow Indians were in the area. Lisa named the fort "Raymond" after his son. Not wanting to waste any time, Lisa sent four men on horseback, including Colter and Drouillard, into the winter weather to inform the tribes that the fort was "ready for business." Drouillard would take a more southwesterly route and Colter would take a more westerly route.

Colter followed the Yellowstone River looking for Crow and Salish villages and hoping to avoid the Blackfeet. The Crow and Shoshone warned Colter that the Blackfeet were a fearsome tribe intent on taking and protecting new hunting lands. Having endured months with Lisa's men, Colter relished his solitary ride west as he was free to become a member of nature's survival story. Once again he embraced the notion of survival and depending on nature to supply him with the food and fuel necessary for him to survive; even if winter would make surviving more difficult. No longer could he enjoy the supplies of other men, but no longer would he have to endure their folly. This was a trade-off that Colter welcomed. These lands were familiar to him, but the blanket of snow made the bluffs and valleys seem new. Colter's new supply of lead and powder plus his favored buffalo robe provided him with the confidence that pushed him west. In addition, during these winter months the grizzly would be asleep and the Blackfeet would be hunkered down. The winter snow would deprive him of the camas root and berries, but game was to be found and he carried some dried vegetables distributed by Lisa.

With little success in finding any Indian villages, Colter continued west along the Yellowstone, moving ever closer to a high imposing range of mountains. When the Yellowstone took a sharp turn to the south paralleling the high mountain range, Colter rode to the south into a deep gorge. At this point, Colter thought he recognized this gorge as the one he had found on his previous exploration. Doubting he would find any Crow or Salish in this area, he reversed course and returned to the point where the river took its southerly turn. Colter now left the river and started moving west into the high mountain range before him. Clark had found the Yellowstone River in this area on his return trip from the coast and discovered a high mountain pass by following directions provided by the Shoshone. Moving to the base of the mountains, Colter could see a possible pass and started moving up through the trees and several feet of snow on the ground. His horse labored through snow banks several feet high in the cold air causing steam to rise from his body. Colter was fortunate that the sky was clear allowing the sun to warm his buckskin and the fur over his shoulders. The deep snow slowed his progress, but he reached the high point of the pass in less than a day and started his descent into the valley below where he could see the three forks that formed the Missouri River. It was at this point he had left Clark and started his journey down the Missouri, while Clark had traveled toward the Yellowstone River.

The next day, Colter rode down into the valley to the south of the three forks and continued his search for the Crow and Salish. On his second day of this journey into the valley he spotted distant smoke rising from what he thought was a village. Moving closer to the smoke, his theory was confirmed. As Colter rode into the village he attracted a crowd of the curious and the fearsome. Colter's language skills and a few metal items he had brought quickly bridged the gap of unfamiliarity and, like his reception the previous winter, this Crow village received him with great hospitality. The village chief invited him into his family teepee where the chief enjoyed hearing about the new Fort Raymond and the new supply of goods to be traded there. The chief shared his concerns about recent confrontations with the Blackfeet and their superior gun numbers and their push into Crow territory. The previous summer had yielded a harvest of buffalo of record proportions so the village was well provisioned for the winter, but the Blackfeet on two occasions had killed Crow warriors and taken their horses, which the Crow had in ample supply. Colter was no Clark and made no effort to assure the chief that the Great Father would keep peace on the Plains and protect the Crow from the Blackfeet. Colter did offer that guns could be had by the Crow if they brought beaver pelts of high quality to Fort Raymond. This greatly interested the chief who promised to trade at the fort in the spring. Colter then asked about other villages he might visit in the area and the chief described the locations of several Salish villages to the west and in an area Colter knew from his journey with Clark as part of the Corps of Discovery. The chief offered two young men to travel with Colter to the Salish villages and Colter gladly accepted.

Traveling with the two young Crow men proved to be surprisingly enjoyable to Colter. Evidently being chosen by the chief to accompany Colter was somewhat of an honor. While the Crow villages and clans were separate, they shared much information. This John Colter was known among the Crow as a brave man with a strong spirit. Possessing a strong spirit afforded a man many privileges in any village if this man was a friend. An enemy with a strong spirit was equally revered, but was to be feared and deprived of his ability to threaten the village. The young Crow men proved to be excellent guides even in the winter weather with trails buried under the snow. The three proved to be a formidable hunting trio as the two Crow would track a deer or buffalo, Colter would shoot the game and the two Crow would dress the animal in little time and prepare the meat, fat and entrails for travel. Before wrapping themselves in their buffalo robes for a night's sleep, the three would sit close to the fire and tell of journeys and wonders encountered in the valleys and mountains surrounding them. Both young men had counted coups and taken horses from the enemy, but neither had killed an enemy nor taken an enemy weapon. They both aspired to these acts of bravery to establish themselves in places of honor in their village. Colter shared his journey to the Pacific and the two men acknowledged hearing of such a wonder, but committed to never venturing over the great mountains as their duty and fate were engrained in their village and the buffalo that sustained the village.

One morning the three awoke to the dawn and witnessed the eastern sky alive with sun dogs "dancing" beside the sun and a bright column of light emanating from the golden ball and reaching into the blue, cold air. The two young Crow were immediately smitten by the sight and proclaimed this a holy moment when the spirits on the horizon were calling to the believers. Their worship began with a chant to Akbatekdia and with their eyes fixed on the horizon they began to sway in the cold air. This was a moment when their physical world received a visit from the spiritual world and in this opportunity each young man believed he was blessed by an assurance that Akbatekdia would travel with them. Colter watched in stunned silence as his two young companions left his presence and visited a place unknown to Colter. Colter could enjoy the beauty of the scene and appreciate the warmth of the sun, but he could sense no more than that. He had seen Crow kill a buffalo and then kneel beside the dead beast in adoration and thanksgiving. To Colter, the dead buffalo was a supply of fresh meat, while the Crow viewed the creature as a sacrifice for their existence and a blessing from Akbatekdia.

Passing through a low mountain range riding horses in the deep snow, the three spotted a village of the Salish in the valley below. Colter recognized the valley as the valley he and Clark's contingent had visited during their return from the Pacific. This was a valley rich with beaver and game that Clark and his Corps reported upon their return to Saint Louis. The rivers, streams and ponds of the valley were inhabited by beaver that were large and possessed a pelt that was thicker than any pelt known to the trappers in the Corps of Discovery. Lisa knew of this valley and it was this valley where Lisa and his men would wage a fearsome effort to exploit its riches.

One of Colter's traveling companions spoke the Salish language and introduced Colter to the village elders. The three travelers were graciously received and given lodging for as long as they desired. The Salish possessed a fine tobacco that they shared with the three visitors while sharing many heroic and wondrous stories of surviving in the mountains, valleys and Plains. The Flathead, as they were called by the early Europeans, had much in common with the Crow and they had been allies in their efforts to protect their hunting grounds from the Blackfeet Indians. While not as numerous as the Crow nor possessing as many horses as the Crow, they were a resourceful people waging an effort to hold the buffalo hunting grounds they had claimed. In the vicinity, there were two more Salish villages and a Crow village. The village chief offered to share information about the new fort on the Yellowstone with these villages. He also offered to organize a great spring journey to this fort for the purpose of trading for European goods and establishing good relations with these newcomers.

True to his word, as the streams began to flow and winter's grip receded, the Salish chief sent word to the other Salish villages. The Crow who traveled with Colter reached the several other Crow villages who were beginning to break their winter retreat. A date was set when the Salish would send a large body of travelers led by one of the Crow who had travelled with Colter. Colter would follow the Salish body with a Crow contingent. With eight hundred Crow and Salish heading toward Fort Raymond, Colter felt great satisfaction with his success. Colter had never seen himself in this role of "difference maker" and "influencer" even among whites, but here there were Crow and Salish trusting his promises and riding east to better themselves and their villages. Each village provided bundles of beaver pelts and buffalo hides to be traded for European goods, including the much-needed guns. The beaver pelts were mostly "made beaver" or prime beaver that had been worn for at least one year. The beaver pelt worn by an Indian would lose most of the longer protective hair, making it easier to process by the felters.

As Colter rode with his Crow travelers, he enjoyed hearing their stories of village history and the bragging of young warriors describing their acts of heroism. These men were accomplished horsemen and proven hunters of buffalo found in the valleys and plains east of the high mountains. Following the Salish up the valley toward the Yellowstone, a great sound erupted in front of the Crow. Colter rode to the front of the Crow contingent and encountered his Crow traveling companion who was frantic with the information that the Blackfeet were attacking the Salish in their front. The response by the Crow was immediate as Crow horsemen raced past a contemplating Colter. In a pitched battle between Plains Indians there was little organization. The origin of the battle was a well laid trap by the Blackfeet who waited for the Salish to ride into their snare. Upon the Salish stepping into their snare, the Blackfeet attacked with reckless abandon. There were no ranks in such an attack, only a collection of warriors seeking to establish themselves as the most able and the most courageous. While hunting grounds were worth a fight, these combatants were pursuing a higher goal by risking their lives.

Colter waited no longer and joined the next wave of Crow riding into the fray. Colter could see that his entourage was outnumbered by the fifteen hundred Blackfeet who were throwing themselves against the Salish. The Salish offered a strong defense as they dispersed themselves to avoid the random rifle fire and arrows of the attacking Blackfeet. This tactic had blunted the Blackfeet attack and now the attack by the Crow further stymied the Blackfeet. The battle quickly fragmented into encounters with coups being counted, horses taken and weapons seized. Colter could see many warriors dismounting for hand-to-hand combat. The advantage of the gun was its accuracy and lethality, but the weakness of the gun was its single round followed by the lengthy time to reload through the muzzle. The Blackfeet had fired most of their first shots and now the bow and arrow was countering the Blackfeet advantage with multiple strokes of death administered by the nimble Crow. In addition, the hand-to-hand combat was not to the advantage of the Blackfeet versus the stronger more accomplished Salish.

Colter charged into the middle of the battle as his blood was boiling. Here were his companions who placed their trust in him. He had spent many weeks with the Crow and knew them as friends in his struggle to survive. Colter picked a central location among some low brush and rode his horse toward this location where he fired his rifle at close range removing a Blackfeet warrior from his horse. Colter dismounted and reloaded his rifle in less than a minute and surprised himself at how little time it took him. He raised his rifle and once again removed a Blackfeet from his horse. Colter repeated this effort four more times as the battle advantage begin to swing to the smaller force of Crow and Salish. As Colter stood to fire his rifle again he found himself lying on the ground, his left leg useless and generating great pain. As Colter lay there, he lifted his rifle and once again brought down an attacking Blackfeet. The pain was now overwhelming and Colter lost consciousness, joining the many injured and dying warriors lying around him.

Colter awoke to find himself lying on a travois pulled by the horse he had ridden into battle. Riding beside him were the two Crow who had been his companions. They were riding to Fort Raymond with many fewer men, horses, pelts and hides than they had started. These losses would indicate a great Blackfeet victory, but the entourage heading to Fort Raymond was celebrating the fact that while outnumbered and outgunned, they had not been defeated. There were many stories of great bravery among the Crow and Salish. Many young braves had counted coups, taken enemy weapons and killed the enemy. Colter had not only survived the onslaught, but was now revered for his bravery and the number of enemy he had killed in the battle. The warriors surrounding Colter now honored this man because he possessed strong "Xapaailila," which was a mystical power possessed by only those who seemed to be invincible. Being near him would impart some of this power to them. Colter returned, feeling fortunate to have survived the attack, while the warriors accompanying him knew that Akbatekdia had saved them from a superior enemy. The remnants of the Crow and Salish entourage arrived at Fort Raymond and traded with what little they owned. They also delivered John Colter to the fort on a travois. It would take Colter six months to recover from his wound and return to the land rich with beaver and danger. Colter was fortunate to be in the company of Crow who applied a yarrow treatment to the wound that helped prevent the infection that would have deprived Colter of his leg.

While Colter was bringing the Crow and Salish to Fort Raymond, Lisa's trappers at Fort Raymond were having a lucrative spring trapping beaver on the Yellowstone and its nearby tributaries. Lisa's strategy of not totally depending on the Indians for the beaver pelts was proving to be the right strategy. Trading for pelts and furs with the Indians was a hedge for his gamble. As Colter and his Crow and Salish limped into Fort Raymond, it was apparent that the Blackfeet attack had greatly depleted their supply of furs and pelts intended for trade with Lisa. Lisa's stores were full of pelts and furs garnered from trapping the nearby lands and trading with the Indians that lived nearby. Colter's heroic efforts were little appreciated by Lisa who counted few furs and pelts offered by the Salish and Crow who had fought so valiantly.

As Colter lay recovering from his wound, Lisa bundled his many pelts and loaded them on a keel boat headed to Saint Louis. Upon his arrival in Saint Louis in August 1808, Lisa became a more respected personage in Saint Louis-so much so that the powerful Chouteau family approached him with a proposition to form a new company that would finance another expedition to the regions rich with beaver. As word traveled of this new company, other prominent members of Saint Louis society invested, including Meriwether Lewis's brother and William Clark. The new Missouri Fur Company would claim the entire Missouri River Valley north of the Platte River. President Jefferson appointed Clark as the principal Indian agent for all tribes west of the Mississippi except for the Osage who remained under the administration of the Chouteau family. Part of Clark's responsibilities included administering trade with the tribes under his administration. The newly formed Missouri Fur Company committed to a commercial presence in these lands and established Fort Raymond as a critical base for its operations and a check on the Hudson Bay Company and the Northwest Company that were also moving into the area as British interlopers.

Colter considered the wilds to the west as his new "home." Fort Raymond was a necessary evil to him. He was becoming a figure of some standing among both European and Indian peoples, but this was not what drew him to these lands. In these lands, he lived on the edge of survival. He fought beast and man to his favor. He found passes and valleys that afforded passage and grandeur. He possessed knowledge of the rivers, mountains and valleys that Clark desired to know. He had no plans for the years that lay ahead, but desired to return to the lands he knew better than any of Lisa's men. Colter relished his return to the forks of the three rivers, not because it was an escape, but because it was an adventure into an untamed land. It was not controlled by any tribe or nation, it was not controlled by any one weather pattern or climate-it was a collection of valleys and rivers that each presented their unique opportunity and fearsome reality.

Colter recovered from his injury and by fall was eager to escape the confines of Fort Raymond. Lisa wanted his contractors out in the rivers and ponds trapping beaver in an effort to surpass the lucrative previous year. Colter, not being a contractor, chose to go up the Yellowstone and down into the region of three rivers where the beaver were plentiful and the land familiar. As he prepared to leave Fort Raymond, John Potts approached him and asked to accompany him. Potts was a veteran of the Corps of Discovery and one of the few men in the Corps Colter knew and liked. Potts was a military man who was born in Germany and still spoke with an accent. He had traveled with Colter as part of Ordway's contingent going down the Missouri River. This contingent enjoyed its trip down the Missouri River to the Great Falls as the game provided for great hunting and the river moved swiftly through beautiful country. Ordway who had been a strict sergeant loosened up as the men under his command canoed down the river. Potts was a brusque German who did not say a lot, but occasionally offered up some cryptic, if not humorous, comments about the good Captain Lewis and the Frenchmen in the Corps. Colter agreed to take Potts with him and with traps in hand and two horses, the two men traveled up the Yellowstone and over the high pass that Colter knew so well.

As the two men rode into the plains of the three rivers, the willows and cottonwoods were starting to show their fall colors. They agreed on a campsite between two of the rivers that afforded a supply of wood, access to excellent trapping grounds and access to grass for their horses. There is no doubt that food was abundant in this broad valley covered with high grasses and interrupted by streams, ponds and trees standing along the streams. The lively, swaying tall grasses fed the plentiful deer, buffalo and elk. Unfortunately for any creature in the valley, the grizzly were also plentiful and Colter and Potts understood that they would be sharing the valley with these hungry creatures. What Potts did not fully understand was the lurking threat from Blackfeet riders looking for intruders into their territory. Setting traps along the Jefferson River would be a priority and a laborious one. Each trap weighed three pounds plus the pound and a half of the chain, which made setting traps in flowing water difficult. Rather than relying on their horses, the two men fashioned canoes to distribute traps and collect beaver in the river.

The days ahead on the Jefferson River and its tributaries were incredibly productive. Traps that were set in the morning were producing beaver by the afternoon. As the days passed, the two followed a routine of setting all their traps at night and checking traps early in the morning for their bounty. Both men had experience in spotting beaver activity and knew how to bait a trap with a well-scented stick. It was as if the beaver chose their fate as traps were being filled in hours. With the success of the trapping, the two men were spending a great deal of time skinning beaver and preparing the pelts. At five dollars for each pelt, the two trappers had accumulated well over two thousand dollars in pelts. Colter could sense "beaver fever" setting in with Potts. He was getting careless in his daily activity by ignoring sensible routines to minimize dangers from bears and Indians. As the two were checking traps one early fall morning, both men heard a thundering of hooves on the plain above their heads. When checking traps, a trapper was on the water of a river or pond below the bank, which stood above their heads. Colter warned Potts that the sounds he heard were the feet of Indian horses, while the less experienced and careless Potts thought that buffalo were passing by. As the two paddled to their next trap, they looked up to the bank over their heads where they saw five hundred Blackfeet lining the riverbank. A Blackfeet warrior painted his face for intimidation. By using various paints and dyes, each warrior created a mask across his eyes of black outlined by red lines, which produced more red lines dripping down his cheeks. It was as if the warrior had already engaged in battle and had triumphed, but with injuries to himself.

 Each man occupying his own canoe, looked to the opposite bank with hopes of escaping across the river only to see an even bigger body of Blackfeet across the river. Those on the nearer bank called to the trappers to paddle to the shore where the warriors now waited. Colter complied with their command and paddled to the riverbank where he was taken from his canoe and stripped of his belongings, including his clothes. Potts did not follow the command and remained in the river watching the events and considering escape. Colter knew this would be futile as they would be easy prey. Colter thought their only chance would be to bargain for their lives with the pelts they owned and an invitation to join them for a trip to Fort Raymond, but he now stood naked on the riverbank. Potts would have none of it and started to paddle downstream when he was shot in the hip by a warrior. Potts yelled to Colter that he "prefered to die here," having seen how Colter was "welcomed" by the Blackfeet. Potts raised his rifle and fatally shot a warrior near his canoe as an act of suicide as arrows and bullets punctured his torso, giving him the quick death he desired. The relations of the dead warrior were furious and drug Potts' body onto the riverbank, where they dismembered his body and extracted his entrails, which they threw in Colter's face.

This turn of events worsened Colter's situation. By killing one of the Blackfeet, Potts clearly established himself and Colter as enemies of the Blackfeet. While trapping in the lands claimed by the Blackfeet was bad enough, this act of hostility was the final proof that Colter was an enemy. A group of younger warriors grabbed Colter and he guessed they were from the same tribal society of the dead warrior. He prepared himself for a painful death, as the energy and enmity grew toward his person. In the midst of this commotion, a voice interrupted the frenzy. An elder member of the war party called to the roused warriors to stand away from Colter. Colter knew little of the Blackfeet language, as it was an Algonquian language in contrast to the Siouan languages of most plains tribes. It was apparent to Colter that this elder recognized Colter and he concluded that he was at the great battle fought with the Crow and Salish that spring. The elder spoke some of the Crow language and told Colter to "go-go away." Colter began walking away from the frenzied war party, expecting to receive an arrow or lead in his back, but this was not the case. Colter's quick steps turned into a sprint, as he realized his fate was not to be a target from a quick shot, but the object of a race for survival.

At one hundred yards from the agitated crowd, he heard a great holler, as many of the young braves began running after him. From what he could discern, none carried a gun or bow, but only spears, knives and tomahawks. His death was to be a death of honor accomplished by overtaking a respected enemy and killed in hand to hand combat. Colter knew the Madison River to be five miles to his east, which he now made his destination. Colter was a man of some stamina and energy at age 34. Some three miles into the chase, Colter's capillaries in his nose burst, causing a blood flow that colored his chest with a glistening crimson. In surveying his pursuers, he could see that most had fallen well back in the chase except for one very young warrior carrying a spear and a blanket. Colter's pace was not adequate to escape the young warrior who was expecting to count coups on this revered enemy. Realizing the fact he would be overtaken, Colter slowed to allow the young Blackfeet to close on him and then, at the moment of closure, Colter turned on the young man. Colter was a terrifying sight, as he turned to face his pursuer, which caused the young man to stumble and break his spear.

Colter then recovered the spear head and lodged it in the chest of the young, hapless Blackfeet lying on the prairie. The young man would know this place as his last and his one and only opportunity to count coups. Colter withdrew the bloody spear from the chest of his pursuer and he resumed his run to the Madison.

Colter heard a great cry as the other pursuers came upon the body of their companion. The wailing and cries of the grief-stricken and angry young men supplied Colter with another dose of adrenaline. Counting coups inspired a warrior to great efforts, but taking revenge for the death of one of their own would create a relentless search for the enemy who had invaded their land. The trees lining the Madison were now rising before Colter, which gave him the hope he needed to maintain his pace, while his lungs and thighs burned like nothing Colter ever experienced. Crashing down among the trees and through the brush, Colter fell into the cool river water, which offered some relief from his discomfort. Knowing the revenge-seekers would soon be upon him, he surveyed the river for a hiding spot. He spotted a large beaver hut in the middle of the river. Colter waded to the beaver house and dived down to the entrance to the beaver house where he found a dry resting place. No sooner had he found this spot when man and horse were splashing around him. The mournful cries of the runners had brought the remainder of the war party into the search. There were five hundred Blackfeet now searching for John Colter. Some searched the banks and surrounding grasses, others went downstream hoping to spot human tracks and others probed the beaver house hiding Colter. As spear heads and horse's hooves broke through the beaver house barely missing him, Colter maintained his position and his measured breathing. As each moment of dusk passed, Colter knew his chances of not being discovered increased. When darkness engulfed the river, the search party left the scene leaving Colter to listen to the river moving across the branches and rocks of the hiding spot that had saved his life. After hearing nothing but the river for as long as he could endure it, Colter emerged from his hiding spot with little feeling in his legs. With great effort, he reached the river bank and surveyed his situation. Some two hundred twenty miles to the east lay Fort Raymond, separated from him by mountains and he had only a spearhead in his possession.

In the moonlight, Colter could see the ten thousand foot mountains to the east and south. He was familiar with the northern pass through the mountains that he had taken previously, but he expected the Blackfeet would be waiting for him there. His best chance for escape was to do the unexpected and the unexpected would be scaling the high mountains before him with bare feet and his limited implements for survival. The Gallatin River was ahead of him and it was this river he hoped to follow into the mountains. Colter did not notice the cool fall night as he trotted across the plain toward the Gallatin Mountains. As dawn began, Colter found a stand of pine and brush where he covered himself with leaves and brush and fell into a deep sleep. He slept until the sun was starting to set and awoke with overwhelming pangs of hunger. With what little light remained, he began to search for food. The pines that gave him shelter now provided him with pine nuts. Looking further he found gooseberries, which he feasted upon. As Colter gathered the gooseberries, he discovered the unmistakable footprints of a grizzly who had also recently enjoyed the berries. Colter shivered at the thought of fighting a grizzly with a broken spear.

Feeling somewhat refreshed and very lucky, Colter followed the river to the base of the mountains. He had no idea where he would cross these high mountains, but found a stream flowing into the river and started following the stream into the mountains. Colter's feet were still burning from the many prickly pear needles that had lodged in his feet, as he sprinted across the prairie. As he climbed up the valley, it reminded him of his search for the headwaters of the Yellowstone and his blind search for a valley passage through the high mountains. Unlike that previous quest, which took him into several dead-end canyons, this valley would be providential. He walked through several high mountain meadows where he found berries, sweet root and balsamroot, but they did little to satisfy his hunger, so he started thinking about how he might use his spear to gain some fresh meat. Before his plan could be implemented, the sun started setting. In the dimming light, he spotted several small piles of freshly disturbed dirt. He knew these piles lay next to several pika dens and that there had to be pika down in their dens for the night. Finding a pine needle bed for the night, Colter covered himself with the blanket expecting to have meat for breakfast in the morning.

After another good night of rest, Colter awoke to the sun's early rays and the calls of pikas beginning their busy day of "haying" grasses that they stored in their dens. Colter devised a plan to crawl to the nearest collection of dirt piles, put rocks into the den's entrance thereby blocking entrance to the den. Colter waited for an unsuspecting pika returning to the den. After several unsuccessful tries, Colter was able to spear a confused pika. Using his spear and a sharp rock, Colter was able to get several morsels of meat, that he devoured as if eating the loin cut of an elk.

That day, Colter followed the creek into a snowfield, well above the tree line where he walked between two high peaks. Moving east for several miles in a bright fall sun, Colter found another creek flowing down the mountain into a valley that lay below him. As he moved along the creek, there were several vantage points where Colter could see the valley. At that point, Colter knew his survival was secure for that river running below him was the Yellowstone and lay in the valley he recognized immediately. He soon found an Indian trail that zigzagged down into this valley. He had evaded the marauding Blackfeet, avoided the bears, conquered starvation and found his way through the high peaks. While he never enjoyed fresh meat again on his return journey, eleven days later he stumbled into Fort Raymond almost unrecognizable with his gaunt face, thin and emaciated body, and his limbs and feet swollen and sore. His former traveling companions at Fort Raymond did not recognize him in his dismal plight until he made himself known to them.

Once again, Colter retreated to Fort Raymond to recover from a confrontation with death. As Colter lay recovering from his journey, his mind wandered back to the thrill of standing over the body of the young warrior who sought to claim his life, his cunning to evade the Blackfeet, and his good fortune to choose the right creek that brought him out of the mountains. As difficult as these weeks had been and as painful as seeing his friend Potts cut to pieces, there was a kind of fascination that satisfied Colter. Colter now realized that there was an attraction to the dangers of these lands, which provided him an excitement he found nowhere else. This was not the forests of Kentucky, nor the rivers of Missouri and Ohio and not the sedentary lives of the Mandan and Clatsop. Colter also knew that his escape was miraculous and that somehow a greater power had spared him. This caused him to wonder how many times he could escape in the future. Was there a limit to Providence? Was part of the thrill testing Providence? Maybe there was something to the Crow belief in xapaalila or "medicine" that protected Colter from his hostile environment. Perhaps there was a God intervening in Colter's world and some spirit was traveling with Colter into the dangerous lands of the three rivers. The perils and dangers of the three rivers attracted Colter and he knew he would return.

Just months later, Colter provisioned himself for a trip back to the Jefferson to collect the traps he and Potts had set before the Blackfeet set upon them. Going up the Yellowstone and crossing the Gallatin Range once again, Colter arrived in the land of three rivers. How could one feel so exposed and so excited at once? Finding wood and running water by a stream, Colter set up his camp and enjoyed buffalo meat procured that afternoon. As he sat by the fire enjoying his meal and the warm fire, he heard two flintlocks click followed by two explosions and the lead passing by his body and cracking into the fire next to him. Colter grabbed his pack and gun and dove into the brush opposite from the gun fire. He started crawling away from the campsite, then stopped to listen for any pursuers. The gunmen must have preferred to enjoy buffalo meat, rather than pursue Colter. Colter's friend was the dark into which he disappeared. Colter knew the escape route as he started the ascension that had saved him before. As he climbed through the trees, he started to wonder about his xapaalila and whether he would suffer a fate similar to Potts. As he scrambled back to Fort Raymond, he bargained with God that he would never return this dangerous land if God would spare him.

After a brief rest at Fort Raymond, he gathered his belongings then continued down the Yellowstone and on to the Missouri River soon arriving at Fort Mandan where he spent the next months, occasionally visiting the nearby Gros Ventre village. In an encounter eerily similar to Colter's encounter with Lisa, Colter met a large party of men from the Missouri Fur Company. In this company was a young man, Thomas

James, eager to venture into the land of three rivers. Colter offered to sell him his traps, some powder and a gun, as he had no use of them. James was newly arrived from Saint Louis having heard Lisa describe the prospects of the lands up the Missouri River. Upon his arrival at Fort Mandan, James was surprised to discover that a trapping contract with Lisa did not include the necessary tools and supplies, so James was relieved to encounter Colter and purchase his equipment and supplies on credit from this complete stranger, John Colter. Colter would never be repaid.

CHAPTER EIGHT
A Kind of Fascination

Pierre Menard joined Andrew Henry to lead a daring expedition beyond Fort Mandan and Fort Raymond, an expedition that would be financed by the Missouri Fur Company. This expedition began under the leadership of Pierre Chouteau and Manuel Lisa who were being paid to return one of the chiefs to his tribe and who had accompanied Lewis and Clark back to Saint Louis. Having delivered the chief, Menard and Henry were given the task of leading a contingent of men into the land of three rivers for the purpose of building a fort from which to conduct trapping operations. This fort would sit in the midst of the most abundant beaver lands in North America and one of the most contested regions in North America. Menard and Henry were newcomers to this area as they led a mixture of thirty-two men who were French, Creole, Spanish and American, with some being paid a salary and some getting shares of the expedition's take. Included in the expedition were George Drouillard and Forest Hancock. Menard heard that John Colter was in the vicinity of Fort Mandan and immediately sought him out. Menard thought it was his good fortune to meet Colter and recruit him for his expedition. Menard's timing was good, for as Colter traveled down the Missouri River he was lost as to what he would do upon his return to Saint Louis. He had previously struggled with this same quandary and with doubts about a return to the lands he chose to leave six years ago. Now he was also struggling with his promise to God and his attraction to the danger of the land of three rivers. The size of this party and the strength of leadership impressed Colter. Pierre Menard was a man of great determination and persuasion, so Colter agreed to turn around and travel back to Fort Raymond for the winter and the planned push into the land of three rivers. Colter had sold most of his possessions to Thomas James, so he now had to borrow money to purchase the provisions and equipment he would need for the trip ahead.

Colter's presence gave the men confidence that their journey would be successful. In March 1810, Colter led a select group of thirty-two men back into the mountain pass he knew so well. Colter was not as interested in beaver pelt riches as the others, but was drawn by his love, familiarity and dread of the beautiful three river valleys. As they entered a high mountain pass, the party of trappers was blanketed by a heavy snow that hid the old buffalo trail and made Colter's job more difficult. They awoke one morning on the pass after a heavy snowfall to see only the heads and backs of their horses. Colter ordered the largest and strongest horses to the front of the procession to literally "plow" through the deep snow. When the sun exploded upon the pristine snow, the men's eyes became blinded by the intensity of the bright light reflecting off the snow. As the men "felt" their way down from the high mountain pass, a small group of men became separated from the larger body. All the travelers felt as if their eyes were about to burst and tears ran down their cheeks. To prevent further separation, Colter ordered the party members to tie together by rope to prevent the blind from wandering off into the trees. The blindness stayed with the men all day and into the next, so hunting was impossible and finding their way most difficult. As the men grew hungry, their fear grew of the unknown and now unseen land they entered. Never having led or commanded men, Colter showed remarkable skill in keeping his doubts to himself and reassuring the men that they would soon emerge from this mountain travail. While hungry and anxious, Colter ordered the men to gather their blankets and hunker down for the night to give them and their eyes the rest they needed. As they felt their way around and wrapped themselves up for the night, a group of Shoshone Indians rode into their midst. Unable to discern the tribe of their visitors, the trappers were petrified to think they were Blackfeet. Colter recognized their language and assured the men that they were not Blackfeet. Colter called out to them in what Shoshone he knew, then in perfect Crow he requested food for his hungry and blind men. Impressed by Colter's plea and knowledge of their language, the uninvited guests provided dried meat and pine nuts. The Shoshone joined the visiting Americans for the night as Colter's party bedded down for the night under the protection of this "Columbus" who was guiding them into the "new world."

After recovering from their snow blindness, the men moved down to the Gallatin River, which flowed swiftly to the north where it joined the Madison and Jefferson to form the Missouri River. After having been separated for five days, Colter spotted the men he had lost during the mountain descent. Upon entering the broad plain, Henry was struck with the beautiful prairie grasses and flowers interrupted by the trees lining the three rivers. The plain was surrounded by distant mountains still covered by snow. The spring melt had begun and the rivers were running fast. As Henry's men descended into the valley, they came upon a field of debris and bones that Colter recognized as the battlefield where he had been wounded by the Blackfeet. Young Thomas James was horrified by the remnants of a pitched battle that left bones and weapons strewn across a wide area. As the thirty-two men passed through the killing field, each man pondered his own fate in this land of strife and conquest. Henry and the newly arrived Menard consulted with Colter on the best location to build their fort. A location was chosen mostly due to the cottonwoods nearby that would supply the wood for the stockade and fuel for their fires. While a diverse group, the men were bound together by the promise of exceptional beaver trapping and a healthy fear of the aggressive Blackfeet.

John Colter was now thirty-four years old and a legend on the frontier. His journeys into the great mountains now eclipsed his fame as a member of the Corps of Discovery. The desire for quick wealth from trapping replaced the political and scientific goals of the Corps of Discovery and the men in pursuit of wealth saw Colter not as an explorer but as an extension of a great enterprise; a great risk taker whose daring opened the door to wealth. These mountains precluded easy passage to the Pacific, but held riches for those first seeking beaver pelts and later gold and silver. Menard and Lisa saw these mountain valleys as opportunity for trapping fur-bearing animals, and supplying the European market with the fashion of the day at lucrative prices. Colter saw these mountain valleys as destinations full of peril that challenged him and now allured him back. How could he return and survive? He wanted to test the wilds once again, no matter what he had promised God. Colter was no longer just a hunter and food provider, he was now a man of distinction and a member of Menard's inner circle.

Travelling three hundred miles in twelve days, the group had reached the land of three rivers. The thirty-two men in Menard's company arrived in the land of three rivers just in time for the spring trapping season. No time could be wasted to start the harvest of beaver pelts. There would be no trading with Indians here, but aggressive trapping and taking of beaver from traps twice per day. Colter coached the men on grizzly behavior in the spring and warned them never to travel alone. He needed to say little about the Blackfeet Indians and their desire to keep American trappers from exploiting their lands. Little did Menard's men know that the British to the north who had been trading with the Blackfeet for decades had started rejecting all skins and pelts other than beaver. The European market for beaver pelts was exploding and the pressure was on the Hudson Bay Company and the Northwest Company to expand their supply. Their London owners were pressing for more pelts to supply their burgeoning trade in beaver pelts throughout Europe. The Blackfeet wanted more European goods, including more guns and ammunition, so they pushed to hold and take more territory.

Menard put Colter in charge of eighteen men who were to travel to the Jefferson River at the western edge of the valley of three rivers. Four other men would travel north up the Missouri River to start trapping. The remaining ten men would build the stockade and do some trapping near their location. Colter's contingent traveled south and west for a day into the Jefferson River Valley. Colter directed his men to set up a base camp for sleeping, cooking and processing pelts and instructed the men on their duties in the days ahead. Colter's idea was to leave a small group at base camp and send the larger body out into the ponds, streams and creeks feeding the Jefferson River. If the number of pelts exceeded the base camp's processing capacity, he would leave more men at the base camp. Colter sent out his trappers and left three men in the base camp before he and the other men set out into some ponds across the Jefferson. As Colter finished setting his last trap, he heard distant gun reports coming from the base camp as forty Blackfeet attacked the three men in the base camp. While one trapper stood his ground against the onslaught, one young trapper ran in a panic to get his horse, but failed in doing so and the other trapper completely froze. With a rifle, pistol and tomahawk to defend himself and the other two trappers, the sturdy trapper faced death and his attackers with resolve. Colter heard his rifle report in self-defense followed by an explosion of Blackfeet guns.

Given the number of guns fired, Colter knew that his base camp had been over run. He knew rushing into the base camp would be folly and suicidal. As dusk started to set in, Colter crept into the base camp. There was nothing remaining of the camp he had left in the morning. The tents and implements for processing beaver were strewn across the site. Two of Colter's charges lay dead having been shot multiple times and scalped, with the youngest member of the threesome missing and presumed dead. This scene struck Colter like nothing he had ever experienced. These were *his* men, now dead. He quickly recounted the day's activity and his search for Indian signs of which there were none. How could this happen under his guidance? How had his xapaalila failed? Feeling a great shame, Colter started his journey back to the fort. Moving up the river into the darkness, Colter stumbled upon two more traders lying dead near their traps. This discovery added to Cotler's dismay and sense of failure. Early the next morning, Colter entered Menard's fort and found a fort on heightened alert if not panic. In one afternoon, five of Colter's trapping crew had been killed or were missing. In addition to the missing young trapper at the base camp, the four trappers who had gone up to the Missouri earlier in the day were missing. Colter recounted his promise to God to never return to this land if God would spare him. As he stood in the middle of the small fort, Colter threw his hat on the ground and announced that "now if God will only forgive me this time and let me off I will leave the country day after tomorrow, and be damned if I ever come into it again!"

Menard was furious that his company would be so severely attacked by Indians without provocation. He immediately formed a unit of horsemen to find the trail left by the Blackfeet and follow them to exact revenge. The trail was easily spotted and the chase began. Late in the first day several horses were recovered and some traps. The next day more traps were recovered, but nothing else was found as the trail went cold.

As Menard's horsemen returned to the fort, there was a quiet resignation in the group as they contemplated the days ahead. This plain did not belong to these American traders and not even John Colter could protect them from those peoples who called this land "home." Colter had never been given this much responsibility and he had failed to protect his men. The long ride back to Menard's fort was a festering and painful trip for Colter. He did not seek command of men, he enjoyed the solitude of hunting. Maybe he had too willingly accepted these new responsibilities, and now five men were dead because of this hasty decision.

Colter wanted no more of this anguish. He was not bound by contract to stay with Lisa, Menard and Henry. He could quickly leave and travel down the Missouri, but to what destiny? The thrilling exploits of the mountains and valleys would be hard to leave. Colter's thoughts and feelings unsettled him. Maybe this land was not his, nor his to hunt and trap. His random and confusing thoughts pushed him into a fog of uncertainty. There was much to tell Clark in Saint Louis and a claim to monies owed him from the Corps of Discovery. There was a piece of him in these mountains and valleys that could not be severed. Colter decided to return to Saint Louis and the "civilized" territory for which he had no fond memories, but he wanted no part of leading men to their deaths and he doubted whether his xapaalila would sustain him in the valleys of the three rivers.

The morning after his return to the fort, Colter's anguish was still sharp and painful. Why had he returned and taken responsibility for the eighteen men? Not usually introspective nor thoughtful, Colter was now searching for some answers. He could find none. Later Thomas James would write John Colter "was now again in the same country, courting the same dangers, which he had so often braved, and that seemed to have for him a kind of fascination. Such men, and there are thousands of such, can only live in a state of excitement and constant action. Perils and dangers are their natural element and the familiarity with them and indifference to their fate, are well illustrated in these adventures of Colter." With his newfound conviction to leave this land, Colter informed Menard that he was leaving for Saint Louis. Menard was deeply disappointed in Colter's decision. He hoped for a long, successful trapping session in this region and now his best guide was leaving the company. Menard sat with Colter for several hours trying to relieve him of the guilt and anguish resulting from the deaths of five trappers under his guidance. Colter's greatest achievements were solitary efforts. Leading and directing men to their deaths was a different matter altogether. Going back to Saint Louis was not as unsettling as leading men in this "valley of death." While it was true five men lay dead in this land, it was the land where Colter had met the most brutal of circumstances and yet survived. Colter was now convinced that his xapaalila would not protect those around him and perhaps not even he himself would survive. Menard now realized that Colter could not be dissuaded and Colter would be leaving in the morning. Menard had wanted to inform his wife of his health and prospects, so Colter's departure would be fortunate in that he could deliver a letter to Menard's wife in short order. Menard sat down immediately to compose a letter in the evening hours so he could give it to Colter upon his departure in the morning.

> Dear Doll,
> I am taking advantage of the fact that John Colter leaves for Saint Louis tomorrow morning to inform you that I am always in perfect health although at the moment I am the image of a skeleton since I do not have an ounce of fat, but I never felt better. I cannot tell you anything new at this time for the prospects that I have at the moment are not as bright as they were eight days ago. The country is rich in beaver, but the incursion of the Blackfeet discourages so much our hunter. Two days after they had begun their hunt about 10 leagues from here, the Blackfeet attacked and plundered them. In this defeat we found only two of the whites who were killed three others are missing and from their possessions we have found we believe that they are either dead or prisoners. It would be much better if they were dead rather than prisoners. Whatever they are, we returned yesterday from their pursuit. I have always before my eyes the barbarity of the Blackfeet-they mutilated with their knives the two they killed. We reciprocated on one

of their who had been killed by James Cheaque before he himself was killed. Our greatest sorrow is that we did no encounter the party in order to revenge the outrages of the Blackfeet monsters.

Kiss our dear child for me and tell him to expect me in July. Between the 5th and 10th of June, I should leave here to descend. Remember me to Mr. Langlais and his family, also to Mr. Pep St Gemes, and a word to all of my other friends, Jane and her family and Brindamaure and believe me for life your affectionate P.M.

If I had known in advance that someone was leaving I would have written to all my friends.

Menard signed his letter and sealed it in preparation for Colter's departure. Menard was a thoughtful man and respected Colter's decision. As a Saint Louis businessman, Menard had never met anyone quite like John Colter.

In addition to Menard's letter, Reuben Lewis also composed a letter to be carried back to his brother, Meriwether Lewis. Colter collected the letters and his few possessions and joined a young trapper named William Bryan for the trip to Saint Louis. As the two traveled down the Yellowstone and Missouri rivers, the slaughter in the land of three rivers continued. After more deaths, Menard's men feared to trap in small groups and decided to trap en masse, which was not as productive as trapping alone or in small groups. Drouillard refused to be intimidated by the Blackfeet and continued to set his traps as a solo trapper. He said, "I am too much of an Indian to be caught by Indians," claiming his Shawnee heritage as some type of protection from hostile people threatened by these Americans poaching their territory. Two days after he failed to return to the fort, Drouillard and his horse were found dead with Drouillard's head separated from his torso, his entrails torn out and his body hacked to pieces. It appeared that Drouillard had fought in a circle on horseback and killed several of his attackers. The mutilation of his Corpse was an act of fear and respect for the deceased, as the Blackfeet believed a dismembered body could not be a threat to them in the afterlife.

CHAPTER NINE
Returning to Somewhere

William Bryan knew little of guns and would never shoot a gun to kill another human. He would choose first to be killed rather than kill another to spare his own life unless it was for a greater cause. Bryan's grandfather, Timothy Matlack, was known as the "Fighting Quaker" during the Revolutionary War when he took up arms and broke from the Quakers in Bucks County, Pennsylvania, to fight the British. He became active in Pennsylvania politics and helped draft the Pennsylvania Constitution of 1776, then continued to advocate for the common man and the development of agriculture as the bedrock of the new nation. The Matlack family members were ardent opponents of slavery while the Bryan family business would engage in the renting of slaves for hire. Bryan's father and the Bryan family were not political, but astute business people who pursued the building of the nation on the principles of trade and finance. Like his grandfather, young Bryan was fearless and not afraid to die at the hands of the Blackfeet, so unlike many of his fellow trappers he was not in a panic when he learned of the deaths of his five companions. Menard was not quite so sanguine about having young Bryan in harm's way. Bryan's older cousin was William Morrison who was one of the principal investors in the Missouri Fur Company and the last thing that Menard and Lisa wanted was the death of an investor's relative at the hands of the Blackfeet. Bryan's cousin, father and uncle had encouraged young Bryan to join Menard's expedition, as they believed in the potential of America's West for their firm, Bryan and Morrison. The lucrative fur trade would not only add fur profits to their firm, but would also open new opportunities for their dry goods business that had been so lucrative in Philadelphia and Kaskaskia near Saint Louis. When Menard learned of Colter's plans to return to Saint Louis, he thought of sending Bryan back to Saint Louis with Colter and away from the dangers facing the small band of men in the three rivers region. Colter preferred to travel alone, but grudgingly accepted responsibility for young Bryan who would carry the letters back to Menard's wife and the other investors in the Missouri Fur Company.

Colter and Bryan were odd traveling companions, as few words passed between them as they walked toward the mountains. Colter was the ever-watchful hunter-tracker looking for tracks, signs and signals, while Bryan was the ever-thoughtful explorer of his fascinations, challenges and hopes for this land and his family business. Colter lived in the moment, while Bryan pondered the future. Bryan would not survive the long journey back to Saint Louis without Colter, but neither would Colter ever return to this land, while men like Bryan would return again and again. One more time Colter followed the Gallatin River heading toward the Gallatin Mountain Range and the Yellowstone River valley beyond. Colter had little time for this Philadelphia greenhorn assigned to his protection, but he was darn sure not going to let harm come to another man under his protection. The warming spring weather was sure to awaken the grizzly bears and the threat from the Blackfeet had already been demonstrated. After walking through the morning and into the early afternoon, Colter informed Bryan that he would be responsible for building the campfire, skinning and preparing the game for cooking as well as the actual roasting of the meat. Bryan could build a campfire, but admitted to never having prepared and cooked the flesh of an animal. Colter was already in a poor state of mind due to the events of the previous days and now he was having to endure a treacherous journey with a complete neophyte. Colter pondered either sending Bryan back to Menard or teaching him how to be a productive traveling campion. Colter chose the latter.

After a vigorous thirty-five miles on the trail, Colter and Bryan neared the mountains and as dusk started they came upon a trail of horse and human tracks. Colter assessed the tracks at fifteen horses and ten men on foot probably two days past. This indicated that these men were seeking to capture horses as the ten men on foot would secure their rides back to their village on horseback. Colter had no way of knowing whether these tracks were Blackfeet or another tribe, but the number of travelers raised his concerns and he told Bryan there would be no fire tonight and no hunting until well into the mountains. Bryan was partly relieved that he would not be skinning game and cooking. Eating dried meat and turnips suited him fine. As the two bedded down for the night, Colter related what he saw strewn along the Jefferson River after the Blackfeet left their victims. The gruesome tale was meant to impress Bryan with how real and vicious these lands could be. Bryan had never seen a man killed, let alone scalped, so Colter wanted to impress him with the facts of their travel and the need to be vigilant and smart. While Colter's cold description of the Jefferson River scene did not keep Bryan from sleeping, it had the intended impact as Bryan pondered how to avoid the dangers of the next day.

As the two rose in the early morning light, Bryan asked what he might observe in the day ahead that might keep them out of harm's way. Colter advised that they not speak on the trail unless they needed to communicate a lurking danger spotted by the other. Bryan wondered if this was really necessary or just a convenience for Colter who seemed to prefer his quiet solitude. The climb into the mountains was steep and at time perilous, but Bryan was accustomed to hard work and hard labor as he had spent much of his young life doing manual labor for his father's firm. On several occasions, Colter picked up the pace of the climb and took the most treacherous routes only to observe that this "youngster" from Philadelphia was up to the challenge. Walking behind Colter, Bryan thought Colter was like an animal using all his senses, looking to the right and left and then up the mountain and down, his breathing was easy so he could hear even the slightest noise or the warning of a dead silence. At ten thousand feet above the valley below, Colter halted their progress and pointed to prints on the ground and proceeded to explain the unique attributes of a seven-hundred-pound grizzly footprint. It surprised Colter that a grizzly would be about this early in the spring, but not surprising would be the hunger of this bear. That night Bryan did not sleep.

The next day the two travelers walked into the beauty of the

Yellowstone valley. Colter spotted the tracks and scat of many elk moving their direction, perhaps earlier in the morning. Colter checked the direction of the wind and surmised that Bryan would have his first opportunity to roast meat that night. Colter explained the information he gleaned from the prints and shoved his rifle at Bryan who would not only be roasting meat, but killing an elk. Colter had loaded his rifle early that morning and now explained to Bryan the means of priming, cocking, aiming and firing the weapon. With the quick lesson over, Colter turned and began a trot along the footprints leading them to the herd. After a forty-minute run, Colter halted and motioned Bryan to move ahead to a pine at the edge of a clearing where Bryan could see thirty elk grazing. Colter impatiently motioned and gestured to his companion to take the shot. Bryan was steady and calculating; an excellent student in the classroom, he had absorbed every word from one of the best hunters in America. At forty yards, it was not a long shot, but a challenge for anyone taking his first shot. As a large bull dropped at the edge of the clearing, Colter felt a great joy that washed over him and momentarily relieved him of the guilt and anguish of being responsible for the deaths of five men. For the first time in months, maybe years, Colter yelled with joy. Bryan turned to see the grizzled face of an "old man" celebrating with unrestrained joy. This was why Bryan's father had sent him into the wilds of Montana and Colter celebrated this moment because an uneducated, simple trapper from Kentucky had taught something to an educated Philadelphia blue blood. After another lesson in skinning, gutting and cutting an elk carcass, Bryan built a fire and the two enjoyed the rest of the afternoon eating fresh meat and reliving the moment that William Bryan shot his first animal.

During the night, Bryan awoke to the screams of his traveling companion who was experiencing a nightmare of immense proportion. Bryan approached Colter to wake him from his torment and quickly found himself on his back with a knife at this throat. Colter's eyes burned with fear and a resolve to survive the fight, as he dreamed numerous Blackfeet were upon him. Bryan yelled his name in Colter's face, which seemed to assuage Colter and relieve the torment he had been experiencing. As Colter fell away from Bryan his breathing started to return to normal, then he rolled over and vomited. Colter offered no apology and lay where he landed the rest of the night. Bryan built up the fire and sat by his friend until the morning light hoping not to relive the events of the night.

While the rules of the trail were maintained with minimal conversation, the evening fire became a time for the two to share. Colter was most curious about Bryan's family and the business they owned on the Mississippi River and in Philadelphia. Bryan spoke enthusiastically about the booming fur trade and the trips to New Orleans to sell furs and buy sugar, tobacco, linens, coffee, tea and household goods. He traveled to New Orleans only once and had found it to be a place quite different from staid Philadelphia. Bryan was curious about Colter's many travels into the Rocky Mountains. He had heard enough from Menard and the others to know that he was traveling with frontier "royalty." Bryan did not discount Colter for his poor Kentucky upbringing and lack of education. What made the Bryan family most successful was their Quaker humility and respect for what made a person unique and how they could satisfy the unique wants and needs of others, including their customers. Bryan asked Colter about his escape from the Blackfeet. Colter was flattered by the young man's knowledge of his exploits and proceeded to describe his capture, escape and return to Fort Raymond. While many young men would have found the details boring, Bryan sat transfixed by the story told by Colter, most of which was true.

The next days were easier travels as they followed the Yellowstone River through the Plains. The evening fire discussions became personal, although Colter was never one to share his innermost thoughts. Bryan's great curiosity and humility gave Colter an opportunity to dredge up some thoughts he had carried with him during his six years in the lands of the Missouri and Yellowstone rivers. Bryan was quite proud of his father and grandfather. He related several family stories of his grandfather fighting the British and chasing them out of the state of New Jersey. Colter liked what he learned about Timothy Matlack, a man of action in the face of death, but Colter did not share Bryan's excitement for the buying and selling of goods. The Bryan family amassed wealth by their shrewd buying and selling in Philadelphia and along the Mississippi River, but Colter wondered "what daring, risk and courage" could there be in these endeavors. Colter had noticed that Bryan carried two books in his pack, which added "unnecessary" weight, so he challenged Bryan about this weight. The two books Bryan carried were the Bible and the *Iliad*. Colter had not opened a Bible in ten years and he had never heard of the *Iliad*. Bryan shared that Homer's book helped him understand war and conflict and the potential for heroics in all men "like yourself." Colter never took compliments well and scoffed at the notion of his being a "hero," so he quickly changed the subject by asking Bryan about his future plans. Bryan shared that he intended to return to Philadelphia, marry a fine woman, have a large family and continue his family heritage of being successful merchants and community leaders. Colter was aghast, wondering "why would such a promising young man waste his life living in the confines of a large city, victim to the fickle desires of humans in commerce." Bryan began to explain the benefits of Philadelphia, but stopped after realizing that Colter appreciated none of them. While Colter could not value any of these urban benefits, Bryan could understand what drew Colter to these lands. Bryan paused and asked Colter of his future plans; "would he stay at Fort Raymond or Fort Mandan or continue to Saint Louis." As the two walked out of the mountains, this question rested heavily upon Colter.

Just one day from Fort Raymond, Bryan prepared the evening fire and buffalo meat taken from a buffalo late in the day. In the days he shared with Colter, Bryan learned a good deal about surviving in the mountains and plains of the west. He learned how to be watchful, how to slow down his busy mind and focus on the signs of danger, as well as the opportunities for food. The one thing he did not experience was the intoxicating fear of the unknown as a solitary figure trekking in totally foreign lands. After enjoying the evening meal, Bryan was aching to ask about Colter's family. It had seemed to him that this subject was off limits, so he had stayed away from asking, but he felt a trust had grown between the two that gave him permission to venture into Colter's past. Colter shared his family history moving from Virginia to central Kentucky and related the profound impact of the Boone family and his high regard for the patriarchal Daniel Boone. Colter particularly admired Boone because he was not content to cut trees, turn sod and attend to livestock "like his father." He described learning how to hunt and shoot from his father and how he prized the family flintlock. At an early age, he would leave the house early in the morning and often travel hours from the settlement to track, hunt and explore, which caused his mother great angst and his father to be upset about chores that had not been completed. As the family grew in number, his trips into the wilderness grew more frequent and started to include overnight journeys where Colter would be gone for days. Colter related that on occasion he received redemption by bringing home venison or skins for the benefit of the family, but his choice of searching for game over working sod would never be accepted by his father. The settlement was a close community by necessity and provided some schooling and compelled attending Sunday worship gatherings. Colter rebelled at these activities, which just added to the growing gulf between himself and his father. Colter's successes in hunting and trapping started to generate income as his supply of meat and skins exceeded the needs of the family and he began selling these goods to members of the settlement and other settlements in the area. It was this business that allowed Colter to leave the family home and strike out on his own, much to the chagrin of his mother and relief of his father. From the day he left with Meriwether Lewis, he had never returned home and had not seen his parents or siblings since that day.

This last remembrance by Colter struck Bryan as odd if not reprehensible. It also created some dissonance due to his great respect for someone who was capable of something so cold and disloyal. Bryan could not imagine not returning to Philadelphia, greeting his mother, father and siblings with an affection reserved just for them. As he pondered these notions, Colter could see the consternation on his young friend's face. Colter chuckled and almost chided Bryan for his sentimentality and went on to point out that his parents had left their family in Virginia and that many of the men in Menard's expedition would never return to their families. Menard and Henry would return to their families at the end of the expedition along with some of the share trappers who were seeking to bring money home to their families, but these men were the exception. Colter went on to describe the number of men who had settled with the tribes along the Missouri River and were living with the women of the tribe and becoming members of the tribe. Bryan considered this separation from the civilization he knew and stated that he doubted any Indian could write the *Iliad* or even write at all. This comment angered Colter, who had heard beautiful chants sung by the women and men of a Crow village, had listened to old men tell of courageous deeds witnessed in their youth and sat spellbound as the holy men of a village gave life and beauty to the buffalo and the birds of the Plains. Colter reminded Bryan of his own thoughts from the *Iliad* that all men are capable of great heroics.

As the danger around Colter subsided, the question of his future rose in its place. He did not like losing the life he had lived for six years, but the magnetic wildness no longer attracted him. Colter was not sleeping well and nightmares were a regular occurrence. Strange sounds and unexpected movements resulted in a lurch for his rifle or tomahawk. At age thirty-five, Colter wanted to find something else in his life. An adventurer like Colter now sought a new adventure. Not sure of what that might be, he focused on returning to Saint Louis and visiting the man he most respected, William Clark. Clark had asked him to find the headwaters of the Yellowstone and Big Horn rivers. Clark was also curious about Indian affairs and the potential of the fur trade. If nothing else, Colter could be of service to Clark and then consider what options he would have beyond that reunion. In addition, he was owed the monies, land and bonuses provided to the members of the Corps of Discovery by the U.S. government. He could only claim these assets in Saint Louis where Clark and Lewis were presumed to live. There were also debts he owed Manuel Lisa that needed to be satisfied.

As the two travelers walked into Fort Raymond, they were of two different minds. Bryan was eager to return to his family and the family business, while Colter had no one to return to other than Clark and no business prospects. Word quickly spread that John Colter was in the fort. Hard-smitten trappers came out of the lodge building to greet Colter and some of the Crow residing near the fort came to see John Colter. There were many questions about the expedition to the land of three rivers. Colter was brutally frank about the loss of life and the tenuous situation at the small fort in that hostile land. As Colter spoke the names of the dead, there were several gasps and a young Crow woman shrieked in pain as she learned her man was slain by the Blackfeet.

Another young man, maybe eighteen years old, stood stunned by the news he would never see his father again. He and his father had struck out on a great enterprise to bring home the furs that would fund a dream along the Missouri River near Saint Louis. As Colter surveyed the looks on the faces around him, the anguish and pain of his failure returned and he retreated into Lisa's lodge to escape the scene. Lisa was long gone, so his lodge in the fort provided a sanctuary from the pain outside his door. Colter sat in silence wondering if he could stay at Fort Raymond for the beaver trapping had been quite good. After brief consideration Colter came to terms with the fact he had not spent six years in these lands to trap beaver. He would continue down the river to deliver the letters that were his responsibility and see Clark. Colter grabbed a full bottle of Lisa's whiskey and proceeded to find some peace and then sleep.

In the morning, Bryan knocked on Colter's door eager to continue their trip to Saint Louis. Colter staggered to the door and asked Bryan if he had a canoe. Bryan said he did not have a canoe, but would have one ready that morning. One hour later Bryan returned and proclaimed that the canoe was secured and his belongings were stowed and ready for the trip. Colter grunted and grabbed his pack then followed Bryan down to the riverbank. Bryan started to crawl into the bow of the canoe when Colter told him to take the stern. Bryan turned and looked at Colter, who looked like a different man than the man who had guided him through the mountains and valleys and taught him some of the wonders and dangers of the lands they had traversed together. The Yellowstone was a fast river and Bryan struggled to get into the main current, but when that was accomplished sitting in the stern required a watchful eye to steer clear of the many snags. Sitting in the bow required no effort at all as Colter watched the beauty of the plateaus and tree groves float by.

The first day, the two covered almost sixty miles as the current pushed the two travelers downstream. The conversation at the evening fire was limited as each man contemplated his destination. Gliding down the river in the morning, Colter spotted a mother grizzly with her young cub along the riverbank. "What splendid animals," Colter thought to himself as the two bears slipped from sight. Colter took few strokes as the canoe floated in the Missouri River and the two continued until reaching Fort Mandan. As the two walked into the fort, there was once again a flurry of questions about the upstream activities and prospects. Fort Mandan was inhabited by mainly French who worked for Lisa and were not so concerned about the loss of life in the land of three rivers. Colter told Bryan he did not have much time for the French and that he would never live among the Mandans. This confused Bryan given Colter's previous favorable comments regarding the Indians he had come to know. When asked about this apparent contradiction, Colter responded that the Mandan were mere "farmers" living under the thumb of the Arikara and Teton Sioux. Colter was glad Bryan was joining him for dinner because he did not have the money for dinner, nor would he pay a Frenchman for dinner if he had, so Bryan bought them dinner. They were in the canoe as the sun rose in the morning and headed into the land of the Teton. Colter told Bryan that the Teton wanted to extract a fee for passing through their land and the only avoidance of this confrontation was to row fast and furious. Colter sitting in the bow of the canoe loaded his rifle and pistol for action and told Bryan that he would have to provide the speed that was necessary for escaping the Teton. Colter chuckled listening to Bryan breathing hard as his paddle strokes were propelling the canoe at a much faster pace. Having passed through the Teton "danger," Colter turned to look at a very wet, spent Bryan who felt he had saved the two of them by his great effort. Colter laughed and told Bryan that the Teton were gone from the river and were hunting buffalo in the Powder River region.

Turning east on the Missouri River toward Saint Louis, Colter was amazed at the number of camps and homes along the river that had not been there six years ago. Ready to stop for the night, Bryan guided the canoe toward a camp along the south side of the river. In the camp, there were eight men and boys who were from two families and they generously invited Colter and Bryan to join them for dinner and the night. They informed their visitors that they intended to clear the land they had purchased above the river on a bluff and they intended to be ready to plant corn, wheat and beans by the next spring. They told of their journey down the Illinois River and up the Mississippi and Missouri River to this "dream" where they expected to build homes and a community for their families. Bryan introduced himself and the men from

Illinois immediately recognized the name Bryan and Morrison as many of their supplies had been purchased at the Kaskaskia store. When asked for his name, Colter responded "John Colter," which meant nothing to these settlers unfamiliar with Colter's connection to the Lewis and Clark Expedition and the Lisa expeditions. While many folks along the Missouri and Mississippi rivers had heard about the Lewis and Clark venture, very few inhabitants knew the details in 1810 as no journals or memoirs had been published at that point in time. As Colter and Bryan enjoyed the hospitality and food of their hosts, they learned of other settlements farther down the river. Colter's curiosity was piqued by the mention of a settlement by several families from the Kentucky bluegrass region. Colter asked if they remembered any names and the only names they could recall were Davis, Maupins, Richardson and Miller. They also mentioned another settlement populated by Daniel Boone's family.

As they climbed into their canoe the next morning, Colter informed Bryan that he wanted to stop at the settlement of folks from Kentucky. Bryan wondered how they would determine which settlement that might be, but said nothing. Two hours into the morning's trip, a lone figure was spotted heading up stream toward them. As he approached, Colter called out to him inquiring where the Kentucky folks might be who were not with the Boone family. The answer came back "Miller's Landing on the south bank about twenty miles downstream." Just as they had been told, at the estimated location they came upon a landing where several canoes and boats were resting on a silty bar. The two friends pushed their canoe alongside another boat and started walking up toward the settlement. Two young boys came running down the path to the river and almost ran into Bryan. Bryan stopped them and demanded to know "where their manners were" only to be told that "he was in their way." Colter chuckled at their frontier insolence, which he understood so well. The first adult they met was a William Miller who introduced himself and welcomed the two travelers to their new settlement. When Colter introduced himself and his parent's names, Miller immediately recognized the name John Colter. He exclaimed his delight in seeing John Colter and gave him a big hug, telling Bryan that "this here was the best hunter in all of Kentucky" and that he had traded with a very young John Colter for venison and skins. As this reunion was unfolding, another settler appeared and introduced himself as John Davis. John Davis was a brother of Nathan Davis who had brought his family to Kentucky, but had died from infection, which necessitated his wife and children returning to Virginia. Colter's mind was filled with memories of Sarah Davis and her six children, but he did not want to inquire of them and bring back any hard feelings that might be lingering from his "failure" to be the provider they needed. Colter was most anxious to inquire of his parents and steer the conversion away from the Nathan Davis family. William Miller hesitated before telling Colter that his father had died in Kentucky several years back and last, they knew his brother was caring for his mother. Colter's face turned solemn and the three men could see the hurt this news brought to a man who had endured so much. Bryan was surprised since he had surmised that Colter would never return to Kentucky to his family. Colter's reaction was not so much caused by the loss, as by the mortality of the man who seemed invincible to young John Colter.

As the four men discussed the movement of folks into this region along the Missouri River, the daughter of John Davis appeared, looking for her father. Sarah Davis walked with an easy pace which caused her body and skirts to move as if she were dancing. Almost twenty years younger than Colter and about the same age as William Bryan, both men noticed her approach with equal interest. As she approached the foursome, she chided her father for passing the light hours in conversation, as there was much work to be done. John Davis had left the farm that morning seeking additional seed to plant as he had depleted his supply of seed corn for his expanded corn ground. Colter had not seen a Caucasian woman in more than six years. He had seen and "known" several women from the tribes encountered on his journeys. None of these women from the tribes would interrupt a conversation among men. This interruption did not disturb Colter, in fact he found it quite alluring. This young Sarah Davis, was not a great beauty, but her manner and swagger had taken him by surprise. John Davis introduced the two guests and she politely acknowledged them and asked if they would be staying for a while. Colter hesitated to answer, but Bryan quickly responded that the two were traveling from the upper Missouri and needed to return to Saint Louis with "important information." This response piqued the interest of the two men and all but stopped Sarah Davis in her tracks. There had been many rumors and stories circulating about trappers being sent up the Missouri into the far reaches of the new American territory. The two visitors were now more than just "visitors." Many of the families in the settlement had been born in Virginia, moved to Kentucky and now found themselves in Missouri. Where would they be in five years? Did these two men know something about the future of these restless families and the territory that lay beyond? Sarah pleaded with the two men to stay for lunch, but Bryan was adamant. As the two turned toward their canoe, Colter assured Sarah, her father and William Miller that he would return for a visit. As Bryan turned the bow of the canoe into the channel, he asked his friend in the bow "if she was worth paddling up stream" for a return visit. There was no answer.

The travelers landed their canoe on the riverbank below Saint Louis just thirty-three days after leaving Fort Raymond. Bryan eagerly jumped out of the stern, while his bow mate sat silently looking up toward the "city" above him. Young Bryan turned to Colter sensing the hesitation and offered Colter a drink at the tavern on Market Street. This sounded good to Colter since he did not have one cent in his possession as he climbed out of the canoe, but neither did Bryan. Saint Louis suffered from a lack of currency, so most of the business was conducted on the basis of credit and barter. The Bryan and Morrison Company held more debt in Saint Louis than anyone, so given the opportunity, young Bryan could reduce the debt by buying his friend some whiskey. Leaving their canoe on the banks of the Mississippi, the two walked the last few steps of their journey together. As they entered the Eagle Tavern with their packs over their shoulders, it was obvious that the two travelers were not "local." The tavern owner recognized Bryan immediately and came around the bar to give him a big hug welcoming him back to "civilization." The tavern owner announced with his heavy French accent that this was "Young William Bryan" from Kaskaskia and then made the same announcement in French. Bryan was almost embarrassed by his welcome and wanted to include John Colter in the "welcome home." Bryan turned to Colter and introduced him as "the man who had opened the mountains to America and the beaver trade to Saint Louis."

Not one person in the tavern knew John Colter nor knew of John Colter. This was not a problem for Colter, but Bryan wanted everyone to know who this John Colter was. After ordering drinks for all present, Bryan began to tell Colter's story of fighting the Blackfeet with the Crow and later escaping from their "race for survival." Colter did not like being the new center of attention, but willingly took every free drink offered to him. Just three hours after arriving in Saint Louis, John Colter was helplessly drunk. Bryan told the tavern owner to find a bed for his friend and feed him on his credit as long as he stayed in Saint Louis. Bryan slipped out of the tavern and jumped into the stern of the canoe he knew so well and arrived in Kaskaskia as the sun was setting. Word spread quickly that Young Bryan had returned safely from the dangerous lands of the Upper Missouri.

Colter awoke alone in a strange room. Lying on his back looking at the beamed ceiling, he began to recount his arrival in Saint Louis and his duties for his first day there. Colter slowly descended the stairs to the tavern he did remember from the day before. The tavern keeper welcomed Colter into the new day and asked if he would like some breakfast. Colter was surprised by the question as he wondered how he would pay for the night's stay at the tavern. The tavern owner assured him that his expenses were covered by Bryan and Morrison and that the tavern owner was "tasked" with the responsibility of taking care of "Mr. Colter." Colter considered this title, "Mr. Colter." No one had ever called him "Mr. Colter" and he was not sure he approved of this new name. Colter accepted the breakfast invitation and focused on his immediate tasks of the day, which included delivering Reuben Lewis's letter to his brother and greeting William Clark. After relating his tasks for the day to the tavern owner, the tavern owner looked solemnly at Colter and said neither Meriwether Lewis nor William Clark was in Saint Louis. Colter was shocked to learn that Meriwether Lewis was dead and that William Clark had been traveling in the East for some months. "Lewis dead?" Neither Colter nor most men of the Corps of Discovery had felt warmly toward Lewis, as he was too aloof, too stiff and too brilliant to be "one of them." With Clark traveling and Lewis dead, Colter was without a means of collecting the one hundred sixty-five dollars and three hundred twenty acres of land due him for serving in the Corps of Discovery. As Colter pondered these issues over breakfast, the tavern owner suggested a hot bath. Colter had no sensitivity toward his odor and months of living in buckskin, but agreed a hot bath was in order. Sitting in the hot water looking at the ceiling, Colter's mind drifted back to young Sarah Davis. After all these years of sleeping on the ground and moving about the valleys and mountains, could he and Sarah have a life together? Colter never thought of himself as lonely, but waking in this strange land gave him a sense of isolation and loneliness that he had never felt traveling in the mountain passes and sleeping under the stars. How was it that he has never felt lonely sleeping alone under the stars and walking alone up deep valleys and climbing alone over mountain passes?

After his breakfast and finding some fresh clothes to replace his buckskin, Colter walked to the post office hoping to find a letter from his family. He had no mailing address, but his family knew that he had enlisted with Lewis and Clark and stayed in the mountains. Colter knew that it was unlikely he would find a letter from them and his expectation was correct. There was nothing for him at the post office. The strong loneliness he felt hours before washed over him again. For six years, he had made new friends, joined men adventuring into the beautiful unknown and lived with the Crow, but now he felt alone. There were fifteen hundred souls living in Saint Louis in 1810 and Colter felt like "the stranger." His anchors to the glorious past, Lewis and Clark, were both gone. The owners of the Missouri Fur Company who knew him were still in the land of three rivers, the trappers in Fort Raymond were miles away, young Bryan was downriver and Colter's family had made no effort to connect with him. Colter remembered that it was his choice to leave the land of three rivers and now it was his choice to either return to Kentucky or stay along the banks of the Missouri River. Colter asked where William Clark had his residence and proceeded to walk to the family residence on Main Street. Knowing that Clark was traveling, Colter still wanted to see Clark's residence and inquire as to when Clark would return. With the death of Lewis, Clark's status and position in the new republic were growing. Clark was now the keeper of great knowledge pertaining to the western future of America. As Clark traveled in the East, the imagination and aspirations of the young nation were fueling much excitement and the ambitions of William Clark. Unlike the anonymity of Colter in Saint Louis, the success of the Lewis and Clark Corps of Discovery was gaining fame in Philadelphia; Washington, D.C.; and New York. Without Lewis to assist, the task of telling of the great West fell on the shoulders of Clark. The proper documentation of the Lewis and Clark Corps of Discovery expedition required a long stay in the east. Clark selected Nicholas Biddle to write the "story of American's great west." This was a challenging effort in addition to the accurate creation of the maps that represented the new lands purchased by President Jefferson. Clark spent many days in Philadelphia with Biddle and then again in Virginia at his wife's family home. In addition, Clark's presence was in demand from leading politicians and the curious who had helped fund and equip Lewis for the expedition. Colter's knock on the Clark home's front door was answered by an older negro man who asked Colter how he could help him. Colter inquired about the return date of Clark and was told that Master Clark was expected to return in twenty to thirty days.

Colter wanted desperately to meet with Clark and describe his findings regarding the headwaters of the Big Horn and Yellowstone rivers. The last time they had talked, Clark asked Colter to help him find these headwaters and others if possible. Now he would have to wait for Clark's return. His other task of delivering Reuben Lewis's letter to his brother Meriwether would be impossible. Colter found that Lewis had been appointed Governor of the Louisiana Territory. This prominent appointment added to Colter's confusion regarding the supposed suicide of Lewis. Colter decided to walk to the territorial offices to inquire about his due compensation for his service with the Corps of Discovery. There Colter learned that the federal government owed him no salary for his service, due to the fact that Lewis had assumed responsibility for Colter's salary himself and now this compensation was part of the Lewis estate. To ensure that Colter was adequately compensated for his service, Lewis had put Colter's service liability into his own accounts and personal will. Colter was deeply touched by this gesture and personal commitment by Lewis in Colter's absence. With the vagaries of the federal government and poor currency situation in Saint Louis, Meriwether Lewis made special allowances for John Colter. While few words had been spoken between Colter and Lewis, Colter now felt a profound sense of loss that this man of vision, courage and generosity was gone. He was told that the Congress had voted to give the Corps members a bonus double of their due cash payment in addition to the 320 acres of bounty land. Colter was most gratified that his outstanding dollar assets far exceeded his personal liabilities from the borrowings from Lepage and Chouteau to finance his trapping efforts in the land of three rivers the previous year. While Bryan delivered the letters from Menard to his wife and Manuel Lisa, Colter pondered what to do with the letter to Meriwether Lewis. He decided to walk to the territorial office and leave the letter there among the possessions of Lewis and inquire about his compensation that was now part of the Lewis estate. Colter knew nothing about estates or probate or courts and as a result he understood nothing of what he was told at the territorial office about his due compensation.

Colter walked the few blocks back to the tavern and his room. Sitting in his room, Colter felt caged and irritable contemplating a wait of twenty to thirty days. He started to think of activities that would fill this time. The first to come to mind was crossing the Mississippi to hunt in the forests he had hunted six years previously. Not only would he enjoy his escape from "prison," but would enjoy the woods and the hunt. He wondered if he could gain some cash if he sold meat or skins in the local market. He expected the tavern keeper to know the answer to this question, so he walked down to the tavern below his room. The tavern keeper informed him that there was a market three blocks away where Colter might be able to sell meat from deer, elk, squirrel or rabbit. As they talked, the tavern owner offered Colter a whiskey on Bryan's account and after a brief hesitation, Colter agreed to the offer and began a pursuit that would not end until well into the night. After a third or fourth drink, a well-dressed gentleman walked into the tavern and asked the keeper if John Colter could be found. The keeper pointed to Colter and the man approached Colter and introduced himself as James Morrison, William Bryan's cousin and business associate. Unlike his brother and cousin, James had moved to Saint Louis with his brother Jesse to start several businesses and serve the rapidly growing town. After the American purchase of the Louisiana Territory, which included the town of Saint Louis, a great migration began of Americans moving from the American Northwest Territory into the French town of Saint Louis. The French stranglehold on Saint Louis was quickly being undone by men like Lewis, Clark and the Morrisons. Morrison told Colter that he had seen Bryan and learned of Colter's arrival and his many exploits and was anxious to hear firsthand about the upper Missouri, the great mountains of the West and the Pacific Ocean. Morrison was drinking at the same pace as Colter and prompted Colter to tell of Indians, bears, white water, Lewis and his famous run from the Blackfeet. As the late afternoon moved into evening, a crowd gathered at the Eagle Tavern listening to this John Colter. Many in the crowd did not understand Colter's English, so a young man was translating into French. Colter's words were starting to get slurred so that even the English speakers were struggling to understand his versions of events in the great west. Someone in the crowd asked about Menard and Henry's expedition. This question caused Colter to pause even in his drunken state. All could see the pain on Colter's face as he lowered his voice and began describing the disaster he had helped foster. In detail, he conveyed the deployment of his eighteen men across the beaver-rich lands of the Jefferson River and the merciless attack of the Blackfeet on the isolated men and the mutilation of bodies that followed. The room fell silent for a moment before Morrison ordered drinks for all to restore the raucous atmosphere.

When Colter awoke the next morning, he remembered only the pain of seeing his dead comrades on the Jefferson. He determined that this day would be different as he prepared his powder, lead, gun and provisions for a hunt. Having "borrowed" some coins from the keeper to purchase a ferry ride across the river, Colter was soon walking among oak and walnut trees studying the ground and vegetation for evidence of the game he sought. As he walked the forest, he was back in Kentucky as a boy hunting. This was not the wide-open Plains of the Yellowstone and Missouri Rivers. Here the hunted was protected by the forest and the approach was more intimate. Here you were more likely to hear the animal before seeing the target. Here the hunter was not the hunted, so Colter could relax and escape the sense of being hunted while he hunted. Colter sat down on a diseased oak trunk and rested in his new surroundings. The only sounds were rustling leaves in the slight breeze and a handful of birds singing joyfully. As Colter's breathing slowed and he closed his eyes he wondered why he had ever left. This peaceful moment was interrupted by a very faint pushing of branches that only an experienced hunter would hear and identify as elk moving through the forest. Unlike the stealthy deer, the larger elk could not easily conceal their presence. Colter pushed lead and powder into his rifle as the elk walked toward his position. This was going to be easy.

CHAPTER TEN
No Man's Land

Colter was growing weary of Saint Louis. His inquiries about his due earnings from the Lewis and Clark Expedition were going nowhere. He did not feel right living at the expense of young Bryan, so he tried to earn income from selling the meat and skins from his hunts, but prices for both were very low and he discarded more meat than he sold. His daily ritual was to rise and walk down to the Clark home and inquire if "Master Clark" had returned. Having learned that he had not returned, Colter would travel into the woods to hunt and escape the confinement of Saint Louis. He was becoming somewhat of a local attraction as word of his travels and exploits moved through the small community and among visitors to the Eagle Tavern. Some days, Colter would travel to Morrison's store and trade a skin or pelt for some powder or lead and maybe beans or coffee. On one occasion, Colter entered Morrison's store and James introduced him to Nathan Boone, Daniel Boone's youngest son. Colter had briefly met Daniel Boone in Kentucky and he considered it a great honor. Boone's courage and opportunism earned him a place in frontier lore that was unequalled. Boone moved most of his family to Missouri where they established themselves up the Missouri River away from the city folks. Nathan and his brother established a salt business at the salt licks near the Missouri River and proceeded to build a road into St Charles where they could sell salt to Morrison. Colter always enjoyed the banter with Morrison and often had occasion to meet some businessman doing business with Morrison. Store owners and tavern keepers in Saint Louis became a source of local information and gossip, as they wanted their patrons to leave their establishment feeling better informed as well as entertained. Colter's day usually ended in the Eagle Tavern, where he seldom had to buy his own drink and where he seldom went to bed sober. Colter's access to liquor was helping him get to sleep, but he was still having the occasional nightmare.

Several times a week, Colter would visit the government's territorial building and inquire about his compensation for services rendered to the Corps of Discovery. He realized that his salary would be settled as part of the Lewis estate, but he understood that the federal government owed him the three hundred twenty acres given to each member of the Corps of Discovery. This information prodded him on as Colter became a frequent visitor to the territorial building. During these visits, Colter would meet with a clerk who understood his claim, but who proceeded to explain that he was waiting for the specific bounty land warrant from the General Land Office. The other members of the Corps had received their land warrants years ago, so the process of allotting a new warrant would take the time needed for a bureaucracy to reinstitute such a claim. As the weeks passed, Colter's frustration grew until the clerk greeted him one day with the good news that his three hundred twenty-acre bounty land warrant had been granted. Colter had never owned land and now he experienced something unfamiliar. As a land owner, he had a claim to a parcel of land. As a landowner, he had a claim to a future beyond the next day's hunt. The concept of owning land was totally foreign to the Indians and trappers with whom Colter had spent the last six years. Colter wondered how a man could claim land as "his own" that had been inhabited by the animals and Indians for thousands of years.

Colter eagerly shared this good news with Morrison. Morrison was happy for his friend, but started asking some questions that upset Cotler. Where was this land? How much was it worth? Would he farm this land? Would he sell this land? Who would want to buy this land? Colter had no answers to these questions. These questions made him feel inadequate and like a foreigner in this land of shop owners, farmers and traders. He asked his friend if he would accompany him to the government offices and Morrison agreed he would when next he visited Saint Louis from his home in St Charles. Several days later Colter and Morrison approached the government clerk and Morrison began asking questions. Colter had been awarded a bounty land warrant which gave him the opportunity to apply to the General Land Office for a land patent in one of three areas on the frontier: Illinois, Arkansas and Missouri. Colter asked Morrison about the three areas and Morrison asked Colter what he intended to do with the land. Colter quickly said that he had no intention of clearing and farming the land. Morrison suggested he sell the warrant to one of the Saint Louis land merchants who were selling land to the settlers coming into the frontier. He noted that land along the Missouri River was selling for $1.50 to $2.00 per acre and Colter thought this to be the best course of action. With his land warrant in hand, Colter started looking for a buyer.

Colter was now doing business with Morrison, selling furs, skins and meat. One afternoon upon leaving Morrison's store, Colter started thinking about owning and running a trading post. While not being particularly social or even business-smart, he could use his hunting and trapping skills to secure meat and skins for sale or trade. The trade in furs was still strong and he could see from Morrison's success that he could trade furs and pelts for common household goods and provisions that he could sell in his store. The next day Colter shared his idea with Morrison who laughed in his face. Morrison's family business had been nurtured over the years and the family had developed a supply of goods along the Mississippi River to New Orleans and back to Philadelphia. Colter considered this and then made an offer that would open the door to his future on the river. Colter proposed to Morrison that he would open his store upriver so as not to compete with Morrison. There he would sell goods procured from Morrison to the communities he had seen while traveling down the Missouri River. This original thought caused Morrison to seriously look at this man he respected for his courage and hunting skills and consider him a business opportunity. As long as Colter would trade with merchandise and have the means to finance his transactions, this proposition made sense and could be most beneficial to Morrison, who knew prices and markets that Colter did not, thereby giving him the upper hand in negotiating with this newcomer. Morrison told Colter he would think it over.

It finally happened some seven weeks after Colter's arrival in Saint Louis. William Clark returned from his nine-month journey to the

East exhausted and so bitten by mosquitos that he was ill. The river trip was marked by several severe storms and eleven days of incessant rains that made his family fearful for their survival and drenched them to the bone. Now upon his arrival in Saint Louis he was learning of the intrigues against him and Lewis and the new difficulties with and among the tribes he sought to pacify. As was Colter's routine, his morning knock on Clark's door was answered by the same Negro, but this day Colter expected to see the man for whom he had waited seven weeks. Much to his despair, Colter was turned away again. Not knowing the state of Clark's health or his affairs, Colter took this personally. Colter felt he had been an outsider with the Corps of Discovery unless he was with Clark. Clark's great respect for and reliance upon Colter could not be surpassed by any experience in Colter's life. He found it unimaginable that Clark could not find time for him after seven long weeks. That evening Colter's spirits were lifted by a surprise visit from William Bryan who was still paying for Colter's lodging above the Eagle Tavern. Colter started to apologize for his extended stay in Saint Louis, but Bryan cut him off. Bryan had heard from his cousin that Colter was doing some business with the family and thinking about a longer-term business relationship. Colter was surprised and encouraged that the Morrison and Bryan families would be taking him seriously. The two traveling friends were soon surrounded by the usual crowd at the Eagle plus a few newcomers who were anxious to learn about the upper Missouri and its lucrative beaver lands. Colter fell into his bunk that night somewhat repaired from the day's disappointments and determined to see Clark.

Unbeknownst to Colter, Bryan made a late-night call at the Clark home. Given his family status and partnership with Clark, Bryan gained access to a retiring Clark. When informed of Colter's visit to his home earlier in the day, Clark was disappointed and made plans to see John Colter on the morrow. Bryan left Clark's home that night feeling like he had accomplished a great deed, which he had. A knock on his door awoke Colter the next morning. Colter was stunned to see the negro who had sent him away from the Clark home so many days previously. The gentlemanly Negro kindly requested the presence of John Colter at the Clark residence for a lunch and afternoon meeting. Colter was overjoyed. He was no longer a man without a purpose, afloat among storekeepers and merchants.

It had been almost four years since patron and provider had seen each other. At exactly noon, Colter knocked on a door with which he was most familiar. The same Negro opened the door and ushered him into the sitting room near the front door. Colter was sitting down when the tall, regal William Clark walked into the room beaming with joy for the reunion with one of his trusted Corps companions. Colter jumped to his feet and both men shared a hug that was four years in the making. Clark pushed Colter back and looked him in the eyes and noted a solemnity in Colter he had never seen. Unnoticed by Colter was a worn, tired man who had been the heart of the Corps of Discovery. Clark inquired as to Colter's health and how long he had been in Saint Louis. Learning of Colter's extended stay, Clark knew that the recent weeks could not have been kind to Colter. They exchanged inquiries of what each knew of the Corps members, their whereabouts, their prospects and health. Neither man knew of Drouillard's death as Menard would not arrive in Saint Louis for another two weeks. Clark wanted a full account of Colter's four years, starting with Dixon and Hancock. Clark listened intently as Colter started recounting his trip up the Yellowstone with Dixon and Hancock and their setting of traps. Then Colter stopped his recollection and with a self-satisfied grin stated that he had found the headwaters of the Yellowstone and Bighorn just as Clark had requested. Clark stood up and began guessing which valleys and mountains were the sources of these two rivers then grabbed Colter by the arm and led him into his study where there was a large map spread out on the floor. Clark had started this map upon his return to Saint Louis in 1806 and had been perfecting it with each returning traveler from the west. Drouillard spent four hours describing his travels and the rivers and mountains south of the Yellowstone. Colter's knowledge extended Clark's map farther west and to the headwaters of the two great rivers that so intrigued Clark. Clark was now back in a canoe looking up at the plateaus and mountains above the Yellowstone. He gladly left any thought of administration, politics and the intrigues of Saint Louis, for he was once again with his men discovering the lands in that part of the new America. Both men were lost in time and had lost track of time and the fact that lunch was to be served hours ago. Clark's wife, Julia, finally interrupted the two "travelers" and reminded them that others were waiting on them for lunch. Clark apologized and escorted Colter to the dining table, which was set with fine linen, tableware and a sumptuous meal. Clark meant to honor Colter and the honor was heartfelt by the man without a home and family. As the afternoon came to a close, Clark apologized to Colter for cutting their visit short, but he had business to attend to before day's end. Clark assured Colter that they would meet again, but Clark's pressing responsibilities would prevent any future meeting from being as engaging and enjoyable.

The next day Colter was sharing a canoe with a fellow who was headed up the Missouri. Colter asked his fellow traveler if he would put him off at the Miller and Davis settlement on the south side of the river. Going up stream, the stranger was glad to have another paddler to speed his return to his settlement up the river. As the two-paddled upstream, Colter felt a great relief to be leaving the confines of Saint Louis and waiting for Clark. Although he had no clear plan, as to his visit with the Miller and Davis families, he was sure they would treat him with "frontier hospitality" not unlike his days with the Crow. Colter grabbed his pack of belongings and started the climb up to the small settlement above the river. The first to greet Colter was a young Miller, who introduced himself and asked Colter if he needed help. Colter asked to see his daddy and assured the young man that his daddy would know him. The young fellow disappeared and soon reappeared with his father. William Miller was glad to see Colter again and asked if he would be staying longer on this visit to which Colter replied that he would like to do so. Any new community along the river would welcome a new man and especially one of John Colter's reputation as an accomplished hunter and explorer. Miller invited Colter to his home for dinner and offered a bed in the loft. Colter thanked Miller for the offer, but asked if he could sleep behind their house as he was wanting to escape not just Saint Louis, but the confines of a room's four walls and ceiling. Miller agreed as the two entered the home where a meal was being prepared for the family and the visitor.

The next morning Colter was up early and heading into the woods beyond the small settlement. As Colter walked in the early cool morning air he appreciated the birds greeting the day and the glistening spider webs next to the trail. The freedom of the moment distracted him from his normal attention to tracks, scat and the sounds of the forest. Refocusing, he could see that he had stumbled upon tracks of a doe and her two young fawns. This was not the day to leave two young deer motherless, so Colter turned off the trail as the deer were "thick as flies" in the woodlands surrounding the settler's homes above the river. Walking out to the edge of a wood, Colter spotted a buck across the meadow enjoying a tall grass meal. Colter had to get no closer for an easy shot, which brought the deer down in a heap. After gutting the animal, Colter loaded it on his shoulders when he noticed the weight of the carcass and wondered if his legs were getting weaker in his thirty fifth year. Carrying the carcass down the trail to the Miller cabin, Colter walked past the Davis cabin and to his good fortune Sarah Davis was hoeing the garden before the midday heat made the job unbearable. As he approached, Sarah took no notice of Colter, so he offered a morning greeting to the young woman who had caught his eye in the spring. Sarah looked up and responded politely with her greeting, as Colter stopped and engaged her in conversation. As he dropped the deer carcass to the ground, Sarah congratulated him on his hunting success and turned to continue her job among the garden vegetables. Colter did not want to lose out to the plants, so he offered to help finish the hoeing before he returned to the Millers. Sarah looked up surprised and pointed to another hoe at the edge of garden, as if it were waiting for the frontier hunter and guide to pick it up. It had been years since Colter had touched a farm implement and as revolting as this work was to him, it did not stop him from looking for weeds to gain Sarah's favor. Sarah was not one for small talk and bluntly asked Colter if he had a wife. When he answered in the negative, Sarah asked how this could be. Colter was taken back by her bluntness and curiosity, and thought about his answer. Rather than offering the heroic answer about conquering the wilderness and Indians, he quietly answered that he had not "met the woman who could keep him happy and safe." Sarah understood "happy," but what about "safe?" Sarah knew about the tenuous nature of living on the frontier, as her family took the risk of moving west. How could this man who chose to venture into the face of danger, to tempt fate, to seek the unknown when death surrounded him talk about "safe?" Sarah sensed that there was something in this man he could not control. There was a part of this man that she only could touch and maybe remedy.

Having finished the hoeing, Colter retrieved his deer carcass and proceeded down the trail to the Miller cabin. As Colter walked away, Sarah watched him and wondered about this man who had a reputation of immense courage, yet seemed so confused about his "safety." Watching him walk down the trail to the Miller cabin, Sarah felt a compassion and understanding for this man who had floated into her life. Her prospects on the frontier of Missouri were very limited. John Colter was a man widely respected and known, but a man who chose to leave the settlements and farming to push into the new frontier. What kind of husband and father would he make? Whatever his wanderings and fears, Sarah determined that she would marry this man.

The Miller family enjoyed Colter's venison at the dinner table, but enjoyed his stories of the Yellowstone River and the mountains even more. Colter sat by the evening fire in the Miller home and recounted his many journeys and explorations. He enjoyed describing the beauty and vastness of the lands he had explored and talked about the warm welcome and hospitality of the Crow Indians. When Colter talked about his Crow friends, a young Miller lad asked about the savage and evil nature of the Indians. Colter took great offense at these questions and comments and talked with great passion about the hospitality of the friendly Crow and how brave and creative the Crow were to thrive on the hostile plains this side of the great mountains. These ideas were hard for the Millers to understand, given the killings and stories shared on the frontier about the Indians marauding along the Missouri River. In these evening chats, Colter asked if anyone had spent time in an Indian village. Had anyone hunted with the Indians? Had anyone watched an Indian mother teach her young children? Had anyone been saved by the knowledge of an Indian guide? Had anyone ever fought alongside an Indian in a battle? These questions were unsettling to the Millers who had made their minds up about all "Indian savages."

The Davis garden was producing more than Sarah and Colter could pick. Each day Colter would find his way to the Davis cabin and help Sarah pick the ripening vegetables. One morning in his typical curt and matter-of-fact manner, John Colter asked Sarah Davis to marry him. Sarah was ready for the question and responded with two questions of her own: "Would Colter never again journey up the Missouri River and would Colter regularly attend church gatherings?" Colter gave the answers Sarah wanted and he expanded beyond her questions to describe their future along the Missouri River. They would start a trading post where the furs and meat taken by Colter would be traded for home goods and supplies that would be sold to the community along the Missouri River. Sarah was startled by Colter's vision for their future, but agreed to his plans. She understood Colter's aversion to farming and his talents as a hunter and trapper. She would grow the vegetables and preserve them for the winter and he would provide the protein and preserve it for the winter. Their wedding was held in the Davis cabin with all the small settlement in attendance. Colter had already begun to build their cabin along Boeuf Creek before the wedding. Colter felt a great attraction to Sarah. He had not been truly loved and protected by anyone since leaving his mother and father in Kentucky. While he had exhibited great courage in exploring the mountains and valleys of the three rivers, he had never felt the safety of a woman who would keep him from harm's reach.

The Colters lived with Sarah's family until the cabin and trading post on Boeuf Creek were finished. The land on which the building stood was not legally registered to John Colter, but much of the land along the Missouri was not held legally with the Government Land Office. The Congress enacted a law requiring a land claim to be at least one square mile and to be "farmed" for three consecutive years. Colter's land on Boeuf Creek met neither requirement and never would. Colter felt somewhat justified by his "claim" as his three hundred twenty acres languished under "warrant" status waiting for the Federal Land Office to issue his "patent" for surveyed land in Missouri. Colter chose his spot wisely on Boeuf Creek as it was easily approached from the Missouri River, was high enough to avoid the spring floods and sat astride an old Indian trail paralleling the Missouri River. Colter had little cash on which to provision his trading post as neither his land nor his Lewis and Clark salary had been paid. Both of these "assets" were tied up in legal and procedural limbo, so Colter leaned for his supplies on the

Morrisons, who sold them on credit to the man they greatly respected and viewed as a good credit risk. The Morrisons' confidence in Colter was quickly rewarded as the furs and pelts filled several canoes in an early fall trip to Saint Charles. Colter settled his debt and purchased salt, sugar, linen, coffee and powder to take back to his trading post. Having secured his merchandise, Colter could not tolerate waiting for a customer and staring at four walls. Sarah took over the trading post duties in addition to the gardening duties, while Colter hunted and trapped. It was not uncommon for Sarah not to see Colter slip out of the cabin early in the morning and be gone until sunset. Sarah's family quickly realized this and would often walk to Boeuf Creek to check on her and provide some company. It was during one of these visits from her mother that Sarah asked about missing her monthly "visitor." Her mother's eyes lit up and proclaimed her first grandchild was on the way. Sarah made her swear to secrecy as she wanted to wait another month before telling John Colter that he was soon to be a dad.

Sunday mornings Colter was bound to accompany Sarah to one of the cabins west of his trading post on Boeuf Creek. There was no church in the settlement and no minister, but there was a weekly gathering of all the families in the settlement to hear the Bible reading and share in prayers for the safety and prosperity of the settlement. Colter knew danger for himself, but here he felt danger for the young, the women and the unprotected in the settlement. He respected their faith in a protective, providential God, but he had seen too much to believe in a God who protected the unprotected. Colter had faith in his instincts and his rifle and little else. Colter had grown to have a great respect for the families of the settlement and a fondness for the children living on the frontier of danger. His concern for the settlement led him to organize a warning system for alarming the settlement of an Indian attack and he created a militia of men to respond to any known threat to the families of the settlement. For these efforts, Colter was greatly respected, but there remained a separation between Colter and the family farmers who were breaking sod as opposed to his hunting and trapping. Much like the gulf Colter experienced with his father, he felt a distance from these people who felled trees and turned soil. Sarah never expected John to be like her father and she loved him for his courage and honesty about his passion for the wilderness and meeting danger in a way she had never seen. John never offered a word during the Sunday morning gatherings. After one of the Sunday gatherings, Sarah and John walked through the woods to their trading post home when Sarah stopped John to share the good news that he would soon be a father. This should not have been a surprise to Cotler, but it was a revelation! This notion of "father" pierced his sense of time and belonging. He no longer was a man of the woods and the frontier, but a man who belonged to someone. Not even his marriage to Sarah had instilled this sense of belonging. He had cared for and provisioned the Corps of Discovery and guided many men into the wilderness, but never had he "belonged" to someone like this. Colter's excitement grew each day as Sarah's pregnancy progressed. The long wait was rewarded with a boy they named Hiram.

Colter's trading post business grew slowly in the winter months. His hunting and trapping production was sufficient to trade with the Morrisons for the goods that he wanted to sell from his trading post. Sarah counseled Colter that it would take time to build their clientele and Colter agreed. In the meantime, he was determined to collect the salary due him from the Lewis estate and the land owed him by the Land Office. He owned a warrant for 320 acres, but this was only the first step to owning land on the frontier. His next step was to apply for a patent in one of the three regions being offered for settlement by the federal government. Colter and Sarah were "cash poor," but they were not alone. Many transactions on the frontier were done on credit or by means of barter. The lack of currency greatly impeded the normal conduct of business and anyone with cash had an upper hand in their business dealings. Colter was determined to secure cash from the yet uncollected assets owed to him. As to the land warrant, the Morrisons counseled Colter to seek out John Comegys, a successful Saint Louis businessman who was active in the buying and selling of frontier lands. Colter had an early start to his day traveling down the Missouri River, which allowed him to walk up Market Street before ten o'clock in the morning and locate the offices of Falconer and Comegys above their store. John Comegys was a serious man and difficult for Colter to fully understand. Colter started to describe the warrant he held when Comegys stopped him and related that he knew about the Corps of

Discovery land warrants and had in fact managed several of them himself. This good news for Colter was followed by Comegys describing the lack of cash on the frontier and that Colter's land would not generate any cash until someone had enough money to purchase it. Comegys offered to be an agent for the sale of Colter's warrant, but neither he nor anyone in Saint Louis would pay cash for the three hundred twenty acres warrant that Colter owned. Comegys advised Colter not to exchange his warrant for a specific patent as that would require him to limit his land options to one of the three designated public domain regions. This made sense to Colter who agreed to assign the three hundred twenty acres warrant to Comegys for future sale, at which time Colter would get his cash. Once again Colter consulted with the Morrisons about his Corps of Discovery salary due from the Lewis estate. They connected Colter with Saint Louis attorney J.A. Graham who would represent Colter in matters related to the Lewis estate. Colter learned that a suit would be filed for his claim against the Lewis estate in due course. Colter was still cash poor. He had come to Saint Louis hoping to buy clothing fabric for Sarah and some cooking utensils and pots, but now his lack of cash was a problem. Like so many settlers on the Missouri, Colter secured a promissory note to purchase these items and after making his purchases he headed back up the Missouri to his home on the Boeuf. Colter made no attempt to see Clark on this trip to Saint Louis.

As the fall colors started emerging along the Missouri River, Colter's calls to Saint Louis became more frequent. In addition to his own claims, Colter's old friend, Thomas James, was making claims on the Saint Louis Missouri Fur Company. Colter had befriended young James at the Mandan fort and financed his beaver trapping journey up the river. James was claiming that Manuel Lisa and the Saint Louis Missouri Fur Company had offered to provide him with the necessary equipment and provision to trap beaver. When James arrived at the Mandan fort, he discovered that this was not the case as he would be responsible for provisioning himself. Lucky for James, John Colter had stepped forward and provisioned James. Colter provided these supplies on credit and never regretted this, as James became an excellent traveling companion and friend. James was not quite so magnanimous as he sought full restitution for the failure of the Saint Louis Missouri Fur

Company to meet their obligations. A victory for James would allow James to repay Colter, but this was not apparent to Colter. After several appearances in court on behalf of James, Colter learned that the court had ruled against James. Once again Colter would not receive monies due him.

Colter's claim on the Lewis estate for his salary was finally filed by Graham in November. As this filing awaited a court ruling, Graham was mortally wounded in a duel, further delaying his collection of due compensation. William Clark had been called as a witness, given his intimate knowledge of Colter's service and the payments to the other Corps members. In a strange twist of fate, Clark served as the second to Graham's opponent in the duel that ended Graham's life. Clark's increasingly complicated life was further complicated by a report that Clark gave compromising signals to enable his first to gain the first shot. Clark stated in a letter to his brother Jonathan that this accusation "has vexed me a little."

Clark's loyalty to Colter was unfailing and his testimony to the court had great import. When Colter learned of his captain's support, he determined to make every effort to see Clark on his next journey to Saint Louis. When Colter arrived at Clark's home for an unannounced visit, he was welcomed into the sitting room outside Clark's busy office. When a tall gentleman with a heavy French accent emerged from Clark's office, Clark greeted Colter and introduced him to Jean Pierre Chouteau, who was a principal in the Saint Louis Missouri Fur Company. Chouteau, a member of the "first family" of Saint Louis, recognized Colter's name and his involvement in the early efforts of the Saint Louis Missouri Fur Company. Clark and Chouteau had been discussing prospects in the Montana area of the three rivers given the report received from Pierre Menard upon his return to Saint Louis and the efforts of Andrew Henry who remained in the distant mountains seeking to persevere in lands removed from the Blackfeet. Chouteau asked Colter for his thoughts regarding prospects in the land of three rivers and Colter's answer was quick and chilling: "How many trapper's lives was it worth for ten beaver pelts?" While the Frenchman understood the words, what he understood even more was the squinting eyes and locked jaw of a man who could see death. Colter's response was so unnerving that Chouteau quickly excused himself and escaped out Clark's door. Clark invited Colter into his office and offered him a drink, which Colter gladly accepted. Clark pointed to the large map still unfinished. He wanted Colter's views on the headwaters of the Big Horn River and its proximity to the mountain lakes on his map. Colter surveyed the map and the two lakes drawn to the west of the Big Horn River. Colter recollected that he had passed by the large lake to the northwest of the headwaters and then found another smaller lake at the headwaters of the Big Horn. He could not confirm that the lake on Clark's map was the lake he had found descending into the valley where the Big Horn emerged from the mountains. Clark expressed his appreciation for all Colter had done for him personally and his nation. When Colter mentioned his new wife and expected child, Clark insisted that he meet Colter's wife and be informed of the child's birth. Colter left Clark's home hoping that he would see him again soon.

As Colter traveled back up the Missouri he considered his plight and his frustration started to fester. His trips to Saint Louis took a toll on him, as he was not accustomed to nor did he enjoy the dealings with lawyers, accountants and government officials. He pondered his business on the Boeuf and his prospects to support Sarah and the baby. By the time he reached home, he was in a poor state of mind and had no desire to talk with Sarah. He opened the bottle of whiskey he had purchased in Saint Louis and exited the house and found a log on which to sit under the stars. As he surveyed the night sky he found the North Star and remembered the nights he had spent in the Gallatin Mountains under just such a sky. There were things Sarah and he needed and things Sarah wanted, but he had to borrow money to buy her fabric and cooking pans and utensils. As he considered these facts and drank his whisky, Sarah joined him on his log of discontent. She grabbed his hand and thanked him for the fabric and cooking implements he brought from Saint Louis. He grunted his acknowledgement of her gratitude. Sarah pushed his hand against her bulging abdomen where he felt the movement of his child. He had promised never to return to the Montana frontier and now he knew why. Sarah needed him and this unborn "owned" him. The couple sat in silence looking into the night sky and leaned into each other.

CHAPTER ELEVEN

A Cabin on the Boeuf

Wilson Price Hunt was an ambitious man hired by the most ambitious man in America. John Jacob Astor hired Wilson Price Hunt to manage his plan for dominating the fur trade west of the Mississippi. Already a wealthy man and successful merchant of fur, Astor created a plan so ambitious that President Jefferson gave it his full support as he stated "I learn with great satisfaction the disposition of our merchants to form into companies for undertaking the Indian trade within our own territories. . . every reasonable patronage and facility in the power of the Executive will be afforded." While the Lewis and Clark expedition delivered a trove of artifacts and information about the Louisiana Territory, Jefferson thought there had been little activity to build on the expedition's success. As one of his last acts in office, Jefferson gave Astor his unconditional support. Astor intended to procure beaver pelts on the east and west sides of the great mountains and then send these pelts into both the European and Asian markets. He would ship to the European market from Saint Louis through New Orleans and ship to the Asian market from a new post on the Pacific Coast served by the Columbia River. This plan served Jefferson's wishes by checking the British movement into the upper Missouri Regions and the Pacific Northwest. To accomplish his grand plan, Astor sent one expedition by sea to the Pacific Northwest and one expedition up the Missouri River. Astor created the Pacific Fur Company as a subsidiary of the American Fur Company and hired one hundred-forty men and allocated four hundred thousand dollars for the enterprise. Hunt had never been to the frontier, but was a successful New Jersey merchant with good business skills and a tenacity equal to Astor's.

Hunt arrived in Saint Louis in September 1810 and immediately began recruiting men and purchasing supplies for his expedition up the Missouri River. He also presented himself and Jefferson's letter to William Clark in an effort to secure licenses to trade with the Indians beyond the lands of the Osage Indians. Days, if not hours, after his arrival in Saint Louis, Manuel Lisa learned of Hunt's presence and intentions. Lisa quickly initiated efforts to isolate and starve Hunt's efforts by contacting merchants and trappers reminding them that they owed loyalty to Lisa and not this newcomer from New Jersey. Lisa's Missouri Fur Company had sustained major setbacks in 1810 and now his beloved company was being threatened by a substantial competitor. Hunt's plan was to start moving up the Missouri in the fall, but Lisa's efforts checked his plan, so he delayed his push up the river until the spring of 1811. Lisa called a special meeting of the owners of the Missouri Fur Company, which included William Clark, to devise a response to this new threat. Lisa implored his fellow owners to support a new expedition up the Missouri to find out what happened to Andrew Henry and his efforts in the three rivers region and to monitor Hunt's expedition. Several owners of the company were starting to wonder about sending "good money after bad." Clark was conflicted by the letter from Jefferson and his own financial interest in the Missouri Fur Company, but ended up supporting Lisa's plan for another expedition up the Missouri to compete with Astor's efforts. Jefferson's letter referred to multiple efforts to transact business with the Indians, so he surmised that the Missouri Fur Company was part of the new republic's efforts to control the Indian trade. After some debate the owners approved a new expedition and a recruiting battle soon ensued as Lisa and Hunt sought out the most experienced trappers, boatmen and interpreters for their respective expeditions.

Hunt made a very favorable impression on William Clark. Unlike the uncouth and "foreign" Lisa, Hunt was an American with an open and engaging countenance. Hunt, like Astor, was a master of persuasion. Hunt understood Clark's goals in trading with the Indians and taming the new Louisiana Territory. Hunt told Clark that he intended to "follow in the footsteps of the Corps of Discovery" by hiring scientists to accompany his expedition in an effort to add to the discoveries of the

Corps of Discovery. He introduced to Clark two English naturalists who specialized in botany, John Bradbury and Thomas Nuttall. Hunt assured Clark that his expedition would serve both the public interests and the commercial interest of the Pacific Fur Company. During their meetings, Bradbury became intrigued by a comment from Clark that the Corps of Discovery had found a great skeleton of an inland fish. Bradbury pressed for more information on this discovery and Clark suggested that he seek out John Colter on his journey up the Missouri River. Clark informed Bradbury where Colter could be found on Boeuf Creek and suggested to Hunt that he inquire of Colter about his travels up the Missouri and Yellowstone rivers as he was recently returned from these areas. Bradbury told Clark that he had met Colter upon his arrival in Saint Louis during May 1810. Bradbury enjoyed several encounters with Colter at the Eagle Tavern and gleaned a good bit of information about the frontier. Bradbury described his initial meeting with Colter as somewhat cold and distant until Colter had enjoyed a few drinks of bourbon. Even after a few drinks, Colter impressed Bradbury with his keen memory and understated recollection of the many mountains and valleys, native inhabitants and the best routes to traverse the mountains. Bradbury was gratified to know where he could find Colter and assured Hunt that this man knew a great deal about the regions they were about to explore and exploit.

While Lisa dithered and connived, Hunt quietly gathered his men for the journey into the Northwest. In early March 1811, Hunt left Saint Louis and moved up the river in search of John Colter. At the Kentucky settlement on the south side of the river described by Clark, Hunt's expedition put ashore and encountered a fellow who greeted them with a rough Kentucky accent. They inquired about John Colter and the fellow acknowledged knowing a John Colter and asked why they were asking. Getting past the provincial defense of a community member, Bradbury and Hunt asked to see Colter, so the fellow sent his son to find him. When the son returned, they learned that Colter was out hunting, but his wife would inform him upon his return and convey the request for a morning meeting on the river landing. Early the next morning as Hunt's men were preparing to leave, there appeared a man wearing the conventional buckskin, standing five foot ten inches tall with a lean build and even gate. As he approached, his years in the sun became evident, as his skin was wrinkled and his complexion uneven. His approach was humble and friendly as he greeted his acquaintance, John Bradbury. Bradbury had related several Colter stories to Hunt and his men and they stood respectfully as the two acquaintances greeted each other. Bradbury introduced Colter to Hunt and the two shook hands, causing Hunt to grimace due to the strength of Colter's handshake. After the brief introductions, Bradbury explained that he and Hunt wanted to speak with Colter about their intentions, but had little time and must push on up the river. They asked if Colter would accompany them up the river on their keelboat and Colter agreed, tying his canoe to the boat for his return down the river.

Climbing aboard the keelboat brought back many memories to Colter and it felt good to be among men on an adventure. The cadence of men rowing against the Missouri current and breathing in as each oar entered the water was familiar to Colter. The Frenchmen rowed as one unit with only an occasional grunt or word of encouragement to keep pace. As the keelboat lumbered upstream, Hunt invited Colter into his small quarters on the stern of the boat. Hunt rolled out a map he had constructed for his journey with the help of Clark and others in Saint Louis. Colter knew the rivers, mountains and valleys stretched before him. Much of what lay before him was based on his own journeys and explorations. This gave Colter great satisfaction that Clark accepted much of what he had heard from Colter and now the next Americans to push into the headwaters of the Missouri were following his trails and travels. Hunt could see that the man in his presence possessed much information about the lands that lay ahead of him. Hunt had no fear of pushing into the unknown, but he did fear failure. Due to Lisa's efforts, Hunt had very little frontier experience or knowledge in his party, so he saw this moment as one of great opportunity. He listened to Colter describe the passes and valleys of the headwaters of the Missouri and knew this Colter was a man he needed on his expedition. Hunt complimented Colter on his great knowledge and he and Bradbury started to "recruit" Colter with praises for all he had done and all he could do for the American Fur Company. After months of struggling to start his trading post and living among the Kentuckians, these invitations and allures started to appeal to Colter. To be wanted is a great thing for any man, but to be needed was more than most men could ignore. Every bone and sinew in Colter longed for another journey up the Missouri. As the keelboat pushed by the mouth of the Osage River, Colter blurted out his decision to stay on the Boeuf. This pronouncement raged against every urge in his body. He would stay with Sarah and his new baby. Hunt was greatly disappointed, but persisted in his inquiries about the lands he was about to enter. Colter urged Hunt to avoid the Blackfeet at all cost. He explained that the Crow were open to ongoing trading relationships while the Blackfeet had only enmity for American trappers and traders. From what Hunt had heard from Bradbury, this was not new information to Hunt, who now wanted to know what his alternatives might be to avoid the Blackfeet. Colter counseled a southerly route by leaving the Missouri River before it joined the Yellowstone River and traveling west into the mountains and valleys that he and Clark had explored five years prior.

As Colter offered his well wishes and climbed into his canoe, he pondered his choice to leave Hunt's expedition. He could not leave his Sarah and the baby about to be born. He felt a sense of belonging with the Kentuckians and the Bryans who had been so kind and supportive. As he paddled downstream listening to Hunt's men push against the current, his memories weighed heavily upon him. He could still turn and join them, for they "needed" him. He pondered being greeted with open arms and a celebration and maybe some lucrative offer from Hunt. He stopped paddling and turned looking upstream as Hunt's keelboat labored around a bend in the muddy Missouri. A great sadness overcame him as his past and future seemed too much to bear. When Colter opened the door to his humble cabin, Sarah greeted him with a warm hug that pressed the unborn baby against Colter's body. Sarah was greatly relieved to see him return and wanted to bring him back to their life together. Feeling the girth carrying the infant, Colter felt even further from the land he missed. He gave Sarah a brief hug and walked to the cupboard containing the Kentucky brew that would help him endure the pain he was feeling. Sarah finished preparing the meal she had started and brought him a plate of warm food that he washed down with the bottle of whiskey. As Sarah climbed into bed exhausted from a day of working in the vegetable garden, she left her husband sitting before a hearth fire looking into the flames, as his mind was elsewhere.

Days after Hunt's intrusion, Sarah was picking beans when a spasm in her abdomen brought her to her knees. Colter was hunting in the woods, so she found herself alone encountering the frightful early moments of a firstborn birth. Sarah picked herself up and started walking down the trail toward her parents' home. Each spasm brought her to her knees until she felt relief and started walking again. This went on for almost an hour until she stumbled into the yard where her mother was working. Recognizing immediately her daughter's circumstance, Sarah's mother assisted her exhausted daughter into the cabin. Mrs. Davis sent one son to find Betsy Nichols and sent another son to find John Colter. Betsy arrived hours before Colter, who walked into his in-laws' cabin to meet his newborn son. At that moment, Colter experienced an unsurpassed belonging and responsibility. The attraction filled a void he had carried his entire life. He was helpless with a feeling of belonging to this little person. He knew that his own life was secondary to this person and he would sacrifice his very life to protect this son they named Hiram. In all the emotion of the moment, Colter regretted leaving his mother and father, who must have loved him as he loved his new son. He celebrated the decision to stay with Sarah and make a home in Missouri. The days that followed were filled with the joys of watching a newborn suckle, open his eyes and squirm to find hands and pass gas. Colter was a gentle man and his gentle arms were a comfort to Hiram. Sarah took great pleasure watching John console her unhappy young son and bring Hiram to her breast at feeding time. Colter did not hunt for two weeks.

The young family struggled to find a routine in their cabin on the Boeuf. While adding a baby to a household changes the lives of the parents, nothing could compare to the disruption Sarah and John were about to encounter. Colter made a daily morning trip down to the creek to fill several large pails with the water needed for the day. He noticed that the creek was flowing slower and starting to rise. That afternoon he walked down to the mouth of Boeuf Creek on the Missouri River and surveyed a very high and fast-moving river. The spring thaw in the mountains he knew so well had been unusually rapid followed by heavy spring rains along the river's course. The high and mighty Missouri River was impeding the flow of Boeuf Creek, which was why the water was rising near the Colter house. Over the next several days, the creek rose faster until it became apparent that it was no longer safe to stay in the house. Colter put most of their possessions and the limited merchandise from the store up in the house loft and moved his young family in with the Davis family.

When the water finally receded after two weeks of sharing a crowded house with the Davis family, Colter was anxious to move back to his house on the Boeuf. Upon entering the house, Colter gasped at the stench and two feet of mud that covered the floor and walls. He would not be escaping the Davis house any time soon. It took another two weeks to clean out the mud and do repairs on the house and trading post. The flood left numerous ponds of stagnant water along the river and creeks that fed the Missouri. These deposits of putrid water became breeding grounds for insects and a source of odor that was nearly unbearable. Soon many inhabitants along the river started getting sick with diarrhea, vomiting and high fevers. Those most infected were children and infants, which terrified Sarah and John. Disease hit the Davis family hard when the youngest of Sarah's siblings became ill and languished five days before succumbing to the awful effects of dehydration and fever.

As the Colters mourned this loss, they received a bit of good news when a traveler from Saint Louis informed them that their claim against the Lewis estate had been settled by the court. Colter would not receive the five hundred forty-nine dollars he sought, but would be paid three hundred ninety-seven dollars, which was still better than the three hundred thirty-three dollars that the other privates received. Days after receiving this news, Colter paddled downstream to Saint Louis and collected his double pay for serving the Corps of Discovery. On the return, he planned to stop at St Charles and share the good news with James Morrison and make a purchase. Colter had seen a beautiful white dress in Morrison's store and wanted to surprise Sarah with a gift. After pulling his canoe onto the bank of the river below St Charles, Colter hustled up the road to the store. Morrison greeted Colter with a big Irish hug and asked about the new baby and the flood. When Colter pulled out his pile of money, Morrison was elated and knew immediately that Colter had gotten his payment. Colter had been selling pelts to the Morrisons, but not nearly enough to generate this type of cash. Colter asked about the dress and was relieved to see Morrison pull it out of the store room. In addition to the dress, Colter wanted to buy some fabric for Sarah to make new clothes for young Hiram. Morrison carefully wrapped the two parcels and John Colter walked out of the store with two parcels and a satisfied grin on his face. As he strutted down the street, four young boys riding horses came charging around a road corner behind Colter. The abrupt and unexpected noise carried Colter into his most frequent nightmare where he was run down by Blackfeet warriors' intent on killing him. Frozen in front of the charging horses, Colter dropped his parcels and turned to face his "enemies" with a look of horror painted on his face. Colter's stance and demeanor so startled the horses that three of the riders were thrown to the ground with the boys screaming in pain. All the commotion brought many locals out into the street to attend to the boys. Others stared at the terrified Colter who now turned and ran down to the landing seeking refuge in the river. As he furiously paddled away from St Charles, two neatly wrapped parcels lay in the muddy middle of the town's main road.

CHAPTER TWELVE
"A Most Remarkable Man"

For twenty-five years Tecumseh had resisted the western onslaught of American settlers. He was a tall, attractive Shawnee with strong features and a countenance that both inspired and threatened. The Shawnee people stood in the path of the Americans who traveled down the rivers east of the Appalachians to settle and farm the lands of the American Northwest. Tecumseh's father was killed by frontiersmen who had illegally crossed into Shawnee territory designated so by treaty with the American colonial government. The Shawnee aligned themselves with the British during the American Revolutionary War, but having been too young, Tecumseh did not fight the Americans during this war. However, at age fifteen, Tecumseh joined a band of Shawnee who sought to stop the river traffic coming down the Ohio from Pennsylvania. Many settlers were killed or turned back during these attacks.

After the Treaty of Paris was signed, officially ending the Revolutionary War, the British maintained their presence in the Northwest Territory, which now belonged to the new United States of America. Much like their relationship with the Blackfeet, the British traded with the Shawnee, using Canada as the base for their trading and journeys into the Northwest Territory. As the hostilities between American frontiersmen and the Shawnee escalated, Tecumseh's family was forced to relocate four times due to attacks by American militia. Entire Shawnee villages were destroyed and atrocities were committed by both sides. Tecumseh thought the atrocities appalling and condemned warriors who killed women and children along the frontier.

He participated in several battles against militia and the regulars sent by President Washington, including the Battle of Fallen Timbers. The defeat at the hands of General Wayne at Fallen Timbers inflamed Tecumseh's resolve to secure land for his people and resist any further incursions into Shawnee lands that were once again established by a treaty. Tecumseh was furious with the terms of the treaty and refused to sign it. Over the next years, bits of Shawnee land were purchased by the U.S. government under terms and prices Tecumseh thought were too generously granted by several Shawnee chiefs.

Tecumseh was not the only Shawnee to see what was unfolding before their eyes, nor was the Shawnee the only tribe being pushed westward. Tecumseh began traveling throughout the frontier, meeting with Shawnee and other tribes on the frontier. His great presence and oratory skills quickly moved him into a position of great influence. In a speech, he often delivered he asked, "Where are the Narragansett, the Mohican, the Pocanet and other powerful tribes of our people? They have vanished before the avarice and oppression of the white man. . . sleep no longer, will not the bones of our dead be plowed up and their graves turned into plowed fields?" Adding to his fame and power was the "Shawnee Prophet" who was Tecumseh's brother. The Prophet was also a great orator who was leading a religious revival among the Shawnee. He preached against the excesses of white men, the evil of alcohol, wearing cotton clothing, and "giving away" land to white settlers.

Now having been driven from Ohio, the Shawnee were living in Indiana Territory. Settlers started moving into Indiana Territory, once again breaking treaty commitments and defying the central government in Washington, D.C. The new governor of Indiana Territory, William Henry Harrison, without authorization from Washington, negotiated with a group of Shawnee a new treaty that brought three million acres of Shawnee land under control of the United States. Tecumseh was once again incensed by the terms of the treaty and loss of more land. With a small band of warriors, Tecumseh sought out Harrison and asked that he nullify the treaty as "No tribe has the right to sell land, even to each other, much less strangers. Why not sell the air, the great sea as well as the earth?" Harrison refused the request and shortly thereafter Tecumseh returned to the lightly guarded settlement with four hundred warriors from various tribes. Tecumseh began inciting the warriors to kill Harrison only to be checked by another tribe's chief, who prevailed upon the warriors to leave peacefully. As Tecumseh left, he told Harrison that the Shawnee would seek an alliance with the British. In addition to seeking British help, Tecumseh traveled hundreds of miles to expand his alliances with other tribes. As he traveled, a great comet appeared in the night sky giving his words and the prophesy of the Shawnee Prophet greater credence and power as Tecumseh's very name meant "shooting star."

To take advantage of Tecumseh's absence as he visited other tribes, Harrison led one thousand militia to the Shawnee settlement at Tippecanoe to preempt Tecumseh and disarm the Shawnee. Harrison moved his troops near the Shawnee settlement where the Shawnee Prophet asked Harrison for a council on the following morning. During the night, the Prophet directed a surprise attack that met with stiff resistance from an army expecting trouble. After repelling the Shawnee attack, Harrison ordered his men to attack the settlement and proceeded to burn it to the ground, including all the grain that had been stored for the oncoming winter months. The battle of Tippecanoe had totally discredited the Shawnee Prophet and Tecumseh returned to once again rebuild alliances and prepare for another battle to secure lands for the Shawnee.

The Battle of Tippecanoe started a fire felt across the frontier. One of the tribal allies recruited by Tecumseh was the Winnebago tribe. Traveling some distance and being in a "foreign" location, the Winnebago were not familiar with the field of battle. They valiantly tried to overrun a salient of Harrison's militia early in the battle and sustained horrendous casualties. The Winnebago gathered their wounded and started their return to their own villages. In a lust for vengeance, they attacked and destroyed the trading house of Nathaniel Pryor and killed two of his men. Pryor was a highly-respected member of the Corps of Discovery, well known in Saint Louis and known to Clark, who employed his services on numerous occasions. The pillaging of Pryor's trading house created an uproar in Saint Louis and along the Missouri and Mississippi rivers. Down the Mississippi River from

Pryor's operations another attack occurred that was so horrendous as to get the attention of not just the Territorial authorities in Saint Louis, but the War Department in Washington. Another rampaging group of warriors killed all nine members of the O'Neil family. Word spread that the youngest child had been "baked" in a fire while still alive. These acts put Clark in a difficult situation. Jefferson had commissioned Clark as a brigadier general of the militia and appointed him principal Indian agent for the tribes west of the Mississippi. Clark still held fast to the Jeffersonian vision of bringing the tribes into the cultural and economic mainstream of the new America. Clark had personally directed the construction of Fort Osage and was responsible for all forts and factories, including Fort Madison, that were meant to expand friendly relations with the tribes along the Missouri and Mississippi rivers and expand the trading of goods. Now many of the previously peaceful tribes were becoming hostile and the British saw an opportunity to check the western and northern movement of the American frontier.

The Davis and Colter families created a warning system using two horns they made from wood. If either family saw or heard of an eminent attack, a horn would be blown with three short bursts. All the settlements along the Missouri River were feeling vulnerable and threatened to sudden Indian attacks, but little did they know another threat was looming. Not long after blowing out their candles, John and Sarah Colter were nearly thrown from their bed by a quaking, rolling interruption to a night's sleep. Young Hiram was also awakened by the loud rumbling and quaking of the earth. As the three huddled together, they could hear trees crashing and birds squawking in the chaos unfolding outside their door. Several shelves in the cabin gave way and a large family clock tumbled over with its weights breaking lose and destroying the doors of the clock. The tremors continued through the night as Colter held his family in his arms and hummed a Crow Indian prayer to sooth Hiram and Sarah. While never having experienced an earthquake, Colter knew this violent attack upon the land surely had to be an earthquake. Colter quieted young Hiram's fears and assured Sarah that this would not be long lasting. Unfortunately for the young family, the tremors and quakes continued for several weeks. Reports spread along the Missouri about the devastation along the Mississippi River and the many who had lost their lives. Colter learned that his old sergeant, Ordway, who had prospered along the Mississippi River, was living at the center of the earthquake and lost every building to the destruction and his land was so twisted that it was useless.

The great earthquake disrupted all commerce along the rivers. The debris in the rivers made navigation perilous and the loss of property brought economic hardships. The Saint Louis price of furs dropped as furs could not be delivered to New Orleans and inventories began to accumulate. While Colter's direct losses from the earthquake were minimal, the loss of market and the decline of pelt prices was devastating.

During these calamities, Nathan Boone appeared in the doorway of Colter's trading post. Boone was a man of few words and after a brief greeting told Colter that he needed Colter's services. Boone was a captain in the Missouri Militia and had been directed to embark upon a mission to secure the territory between Fort Madison and Saint Louis and prevent British and Indian incursions such as had occurred at Pryor's trading post and the O'Neil family massacre. The growing threat from the north required a strong response by the Missouri Militia as Tecumseh and his allies schemed with the British to take territory back from the frontier settlers. To accomplish this, Clark worked with Louisiana Territory Governor Benjamin Howard to devise a scheme to build a series of forts and blockhouses along the Mississippi River that would impede any forays toward Saint Louis and hold ground at Fort Madison. Clark, the realist, knew he would receive no support from Washington, given the pending war with the British in the East, so he called out the local militia, including a unit of mounted rangers commanded by Boone.

Colter was the perfect choice. He had experience building frontier forts, could shoot an elk at one hundred fifty yards, and was fearless. Having Colter serve in his militia unit would bolster Boone's recruiting efforts and lend status to his detachment of rangers. While Colter never really understood this, he was a man held in high esteem. In some ways, not even Daniel Boone was held in as high regard as Colter who had traveled so far and so fearlessly to expand the frontier of the new republic and now lived so humbly. Colter told Boone that he was honored by the request and asked how many months he would be assigned to this unit. Boone indicated that he required three months of service from each enlistment and another three months at the discretion of the commanding officer. Colter responded that he would consider it and discuss it with his young wife.

Colter had served in the Kentucky militia and understood several things about serving in a militia unit. The pay was less than that of the regular army; he would have to provision himself with food, powder and a horse, and there would be no retirement benefits from his service. To leave his family for up to six months would require someone to care for his young family. Beyond food and shelter, there was the constant threat of disease and marauding Indians that needed to be addressed. Sarah spoke with her father and mother about Nathan Boone's request. They already knew about Boone's recruiting, as Boone had asked one of the Davis sons to join his rangers. The Davis family embraced the frontier code of mutual aid and mutual protection and did not hesitate to encourage son and daughter to agree to the proposed hardship and separation that was necessary for the protection of those living on the frontier. Sarah shared her parents' decision with Colter, but both wondered how Colter would finance his service given their poor finances. Colter responded that he would ask William Clark for a loan to buy his horse and supplies. Sarah agreed to this plan.

The next day Colter set out for Saint Louis. The river was flowing with debris from the earthquakes, which made canoeing down the river perilous. The Boone's Lick road was littered with fallen trees and rock slides, so Colter chose to risk the river route. When he arrived in Saint Louis he was amazed by the damage to homes and buildings. Very few chimneys survived the quakes, so the streets were littered with bricks, and several buildings on Market Street had fallen. The town was alive with the sounds of saws, hammers and mules pulling debris and lumber. As he walked up Main Street toward Clark's house, he recounted his last visit there and how distracted Clark seemed to be. Colter also wondered about Clark's progress on his map. As the door opened, there stood the familiar Negro who had sent him away on several occasions in the past. This time the kindly gentleman recognized Colter and invited him into the vestibule and then disappeared to inform General Clark of Colter's presence.

After a brief wait, the tall, red-haired Kentuckian appeared and warmly greeted Colter. Clark apologized for having little time to spend with Colter, but invited him into his receiving room where Clark inquired about Colter's family and how they had faired in the recent earthquakes. Clark was relieved to hear that the Colter and Davis families had escaped the great losses incurred by many. Clark conveyed that he had urged Nathan Boone to recruit Colter and encouraged Colter to accept. This gave Colter the opening he was hoping to get, so he proposed a loan of forty-five dollars for provisioning his services and buying a mount. Clark did not hesitate to agree to make the loan and generously did not stipulate the terms of repayment. Colter sat back in his chair relieved by Clark's response and generosity. Clark wrote the necessary script for Colter and got up from his chair behind the desk. Colter took this as his signal to depart, but before he could get to the door, Clark caught him by the arm. Standing several inches taller than Colter, who was five feet ten inches tall, and being a few years older than Colter, Clark paused to consider the words he wanted to share with Colter. "John, I have asked much of you since we first met and now I am in your debt once again. No one performed their duty more honorably while serving in the Corps of Discovery and I see once again you are choosing to serve at great risk to yourself and without fanfare. My deepest gratitude and good wishes go with you." Colter found the moment uncomfortable and somewhat embarrassing. He offered a quick, "Always willing to serve you, General, and thanks for the loan." As he walked back down Main Street, he thought back on his confrontation with Drouillard and the calm, understanding intervention by Clark.

On his return home, Colter stopped at the Boone's settlement along the river. He had never visited the Boone home and was impressed as he walked up to the stately two story Georgian home. Colter concluded that the salt business had been good to the Boones. Colter approached a young boy and asked to see Nathan Boone. Soon Captain Boone appeared and was happy to see Colter on his porch. Learning of Colter's decision to join his command gave Boone the boost he needed to fill out his ranks and start planning for the work ahead. Boone informed Colter of his necessary provisions and then surprised him with the offer of a fine horse to use during his enlistment as a ranger. He was to report for duty on March 3, 1812, when he would be enlisted as a private in the Missouri Rangers, which suited him fine as he wanted never again to command men in the face of danger. Colter's pay would be one dollar per day served.

There were four different fortifications being built on the frontier, all for the purpose of providing protection from the Indians and some for the purpose of facilitating trade with the Indians. Many frontier families chose to fortify their own homes, including adding gun holes from which to fire upon attacking Indians. A second type of fortification was a four-walled, square blockhouse of two to three floors with numerous holes from which to fire upon attacking Indians. In addition to the blockhouse, there was often a barracks or out-buildings where residents could live and work and retreat to the blockhouse when attacked. The third type of fortification was the factory fort that served both trading and defensive purposes. This fort often included a perimeter stockade that enclosed blockhouses, trading grounds, storage buildings and barracks. Fort Osage and Fort Madison were fortifications of this type. The fourth type of fortification was the cantonment that existed in Saint Louis where multiple buildings and structures housed a large contingent of regular army and government officials behind a well-fortified stockade. In addition to patrolling and intercepting hostile Indians, Captain Boone's Rangers were to build the second type of fortification that could be built quickly and offer stiff resistance to any attack from behind the walls of a blockhouse.

On March 3, Colter reported to duty in St Charles where Boone's forty-one men were gathering. James Morrison was desperately looking for his friend John Colter among the men gathering there near his store. He had heard from Boone that Colter agreed to serve in his unit. Like all the residents of St Charles, Morrison and his family were living with the fear of a sudden Indian attack. In addition to this fear, Morrison's business was suffering badly from the dislocations of the earthquakes and flight from the Indians. Some settlers were leaving the river valley, while others hunkered down, avoiding travel into St Charles where they might conduct business with Morrison. Upon finding Colter, Morrison stopped and suddenly realized that John Colter had risked his life in so many ways and much to the benefit of the Morrison and Bryan families.

Morrison challenged Colter about his decision asking, even pleading, that he reconsider his decision. Colter was among the oldest gathered there on the St Charles green and Morrison pointed this out to him. Colter chuckled at this observation saying that this had been the case for most of his years traveling the frontier and that he could still outrun the Blackfeet if he had to. Morrison laughed and grabbed his friend for a mighty Irish hug that conveyed genuine affection and respect for a man he found so courageous, yet unassuming. Little did Morrison know, that he would never again buy a drink for his friend, John Colter.

As the names were read and the troops mustered in, various responses were heard from the crowd gathered around the Missouri Rangers. For some, large families offered a "huzzah" and for other recruits there was but a whimper from a young wife fearful for her husband. Colter heard neither. He had forbidden Sarah and the Davis family from traveling down the perilous Missouri River for this ceremony. Colter had neither seen nor heard from his parents and siblings in nine years. He made no effort to seek them out nor had they made any effort to communicate with him knowing that he had joined the Corps of Discovery. While it was plausible that they thought him perished on his journey to the Pacific, enough word had travelled along the frontier that they must have known he survived. Perhaps they knew of his decision to turn back into the land of three rivers and expected him to perish there. Or perhaps it was just the culture of the frontier; that certain men would be required to leave their families and confront death for the greater purpose of conquering the West so that families and farmers could flourish.

On March 19, Boone's mounted Rangers moved east toward Saint Louis then turned north along the Mississippi toward Fort Madison. As the Rangers rode north, many of the privates pushed along the line to ride near John Colter. Many of the recruits were half Colter's age, but most knew of Colter's adventures. One young private rode up beside Colter and asked if he had ever scalped an Indian. Colter replied that he had never scalped an Indian and that he had lived more days among Indians and walked more miles with Indians than he had fought battles with Indians. Another young private asked about a necklace that Colter wore around his neck. The young man marveled at the gold and silver beads around Colter's neck. Colter explained that his necklace was a gift from a Crow chief who had traded two horses for this necklace, which was made by the Navajo far to the southwest. One incensed private had heard enough about these Indian "tales" and reminded all within hearing that Indians had "slaughtered" the O'Neil family just days before and that Indians were "savages needing to be burned for their atrocities." Colter offered no objection and rode on.

The atrocities committed in Ralls County brought the Rangers north to an area near Salt River, which was a Mississippi River tributary. Governor Howard of the Louisiana Territory wanted the Rangers posted in this area because it was the area of the attack, but was also a crossing point on the Mississippi. Nathan Boone was already in the area with a small contingent of men surveying the land for an ideal fort position from which to defend the area. Boone selected a promontory above the Mississippi lowlands that could command the river and movements along the west bank of the river. This position would be ideal for protecting Saint Louis should Fort Madison be overcome and Indian and British intruders move south. The evidence was growing that the British were engaging many tribes for trade and ultimately alliances. In addition, Tecumseh was actively recruiting other tribes for his confederacy.

Boone's plan was to build the blockhouse using part of his troop and send the rest of the men on patrols looking for hostiles. Distinguishing hostile from friendly Indian was becoming a major challenge for the militia and the territorial government. On several occasions, militia had attacked friendly Indian villages, which pushed the surviving friendly Indians into the lap of Tecumseh and the British. To protect the friendly tribes, Clark urged all tribes that were friendly toward the Americans to move south of a line running from Fort Madison on the Mississippi River to Fort Osage on the Missouri River. Moving south of this line or even planning to move south of this line caused hostile Indians to attack the tribes they thought were being disloyal to the Indian cause. The blockhouse to be built would be both a position from which to protect American settlers and Indians friendly to the U.S government. Boone chose Colter to help direct the blockhouse construction given his experience. There was an ample supply of good timber for the construction project. All the men had felled trees and helped build homes and stockades, so they knew what good timber looked like and were proficient at cutting down trees. There were three crews involved in the effort: those cutting down the trees, those stripping and hewing the logs and those preparing the site and erecting the building. While Colter had participated in building several forts along the Missouri and Yellowstone, he had never helped build a blockhouse. Several of Boone's men had helped build Fort Osage and several other blockhouses, so these men were assigned to the site crew. Colter was assigned to the log preparation crew. Each log had to be debarked and hewn flat which was critical to the fit of the logs and the security of the occupants during an attack. It was all backbreaking work and the young recruits working alongside Colter were amazed at his strength and stamina.

After several weeks of work, the blockhouse was almost complete and John Colter was slowing down as his strength and stamina were failing. Colter pushed himself, but needed to take more respites as he experienced tremendous back pain, which he attributed to his ax work. One night he suffered from chills that shook his body and he became very nauseated. The next morning, he tried to join his crew, but everyone around him could see that Colter was very sick. The lieutenant supervising Colter's crew told him to return to his tent. Colter spent the day shaking from fever and vomiting anything he put in his stomach. These symptoms went on for three days, then he started to feel better. He reported for work in the morning, but he was quite weak from his lack of nourishment and sleep. He was able to help finish a couple of logs, but all could see that he was clearly not himself. That night the fever returned and he started experiencing an extreme amount of abdominal pain. His lieutenant issued several drams of whiskey to help Colter get some relief from the pain. The next morning it was apparent that Colter would not be able to join his crew. The fever took over his body and the nausea was constant. The abdominal pain was a symptom of his liver beginning to fail, which yellowed his skin and his eyes.

Colter began to hallucinate. From beyond his tent, the men could hear him yelling to Potts to drop his gun, followed by Colter's groans as Potts was hacked to pieces on the bank of the Jefferson River. This event was relived several times, then followed by Colter's warning his men to stay together and warning them to break from setting traps and survey the area for Blackfeet. As the fever raged, Colter pleaded with his son, Hiram, not to leave Sarah as Colter had left his mother. He pleaded with Hiram to be strong and wait for his father to return. On several occasions, Colter "reported to duty" in the presence of General Clark, asking Clark if he should take young Shannon with him for the day.

On June 4, 1812, Sarah Colter received a letter personally delivered by a young private in the Missouri Rangers.

> Dear Madam Colter,
>
> It is with great sorrow that I regret to inform you of the death of your husband, John Colter, on May 7, 1812, while serving as a private in the Missouri Rangers unit under my command. While serving his unit briefly, he served bravely and diligently, which was his manner for the years I knew him. He died from jaundice after a brief illness while serving near the Mississippi River.
>
> Your husband was a most remarkable man. I am well acquainted with the hardships and dangers of travel in the regions along the Missouri and Mississippi rivers, so I have great admiration for the courageous efforts of your husband to serve his country and all those who asked so much of him. He was a quiet man not prone to boast or promote himself for selfish gain and yet having accomplished so much for which he could boast.
>
> Please accept my most sincere condolences and the appreciation of the Missouri Rangers, the Governor of the Louisiana Territory and the President of the United States.
>
> Nathan Boone
> Captain Missouri Rangers

Sources Used in Writing This Book

This book is an historical novel that focuses on the life of John Colter who lived during the dawning of the United States of America. Every effort was made to accurately convey what is known of John Colter and the people and events that shaped his life. Colter kept no journal and no letters penned by Colter have been found. Fortunately, many of those people who knew Colter and travelled those many miles with him were prolific and these people writing their own journals and books provided most of the historical information used in writing this book. In addition, numerous sources were used regarding the economic, social and political setting for Colter's life. Colter has had several credible and devoted biographers who also helped "fill in some of the blanks" regarding Colter's life and travels. One noteworthy historical effort is the work of Ronald M. Anglin and Larry E. Morris who among other things provided a compelling suggested route of Colter when he first visited modern day Yellowstone Park. There is ongoing research and discourse regarding many facts of Colter's life including his birth place, his burial location, his marriage, several of his travel routes and the years spent in Montana and Wyoming.

One advantage of the historical novelist is the freedom to take known relationships and develop a deeper, yet hypothetical, understanding of the relationship and the character and personality of the individuals involved. Examples found in this book are the relationships of Colter with William Clark, young William Bryan and his family, Forrest Hancock, Sargent John Ordway, George Drouillard, Nathan Boone, John Potts and Thomas James. In addition, several fictitious characters from the native peoples were introduced to describe Colter's relationship with the many native people encountered during his travels. Every attempt was made to present a balanced description of the often cruel and tragic relationship between the resident native peoples and the Americans who entered their world.

History of the Expedition Under the Command of Captains Lewis and Clark, Volumes 1 and 2 by Meriwether Lewis, William Clark and Nicholas Biddle

Discovering Lewis and Clark Website, Lewis & Clark Fort Mandan Foundation, Lewis & Clark Trail Foundation, National Park Service Lewis and Clark National Historic Trail,

The Journals of the Lewis and Clark Expedition, edited by Gary E. Moulton, 13 vols, (Lincoln: University of Nebraska Press, 1983-2001)

"Discovering John Colter" by Timothy Forrest Coulter, We Proceed on, May 2014

Transcript: Jefferson's Instructions for Meriwether Lewis, "Thomas Jefferson and Early Western Explorers," Transcribed and Edited by Gerard W. Gawalt, Manuscript Division, Library of Congress

"Lewis and Clark: Wooing The Sioux," by Sammye J. Meadows, Jana Prewitt, Lewis and Clark for Dummies

"The Formative Years, 1783-1812," American Military History, Office of the Chief of the Military History, United States Army,(Washington D.C., Center of Military History, 1989)

A History of Methodism in Kentucky: Volume 1 from 1783 to 1820, by W. E. Arnold, First Fruits Press, 2012

"Fashionable Felted Fur," and "A Brief History of the Beaver Trade," by Kelly Feinstein, History Department, UC Santa Cruz, March 2006

"Russian Expansion to America," by Stephen Watrous excerpted from 1998 Fort Ross Interpretive Association (Fort Ross Conservancy)

"Firearms of the Lewis and Clark Expedition: A Summary," by S. K. Wier

"Settlers," Franklin County, Missouri Genealogy Trails from Goodspeed's Franklin County History, 1888, Goodspeed Publishing Co. Transcribed by : Barb Z. 2009

"Journal of a Voyage up the Missouri River in 1811," by Henry Marie Brackenridge, published by Cramer, Spear and Eichbaum, Pittsburgh, 1814.

Collections of the Kansas State Historical Society, Volume 10 "Floods in the Missouri River"

Letters Received by Secretary of War Relating to Indian Affairs, 1800-1816, U.S. National Archives microcopy No. 271 (1959)

"French Entrepreneurship in the Post Colonial Fur Trade," by B. Pierre Lebeau, North Central College, Naperville, Illinois

Louisiana Gazette, St Louis

Selected Papers of the 2010 Fur Trade Symposium at the Three Forks, Edited by Jim Hardee, Published by Three Forks Area Historical Society, 2011

Dear Brother, Letter of William Clark to Jonathan Clark, Edited by James J. Holmberg, Yale University Press, New Haven & London, 2002

St Louis Circuit Court Papers, Meriwether Lewis Papers and St Louis Fur Company Record Books, 1809-1812, Missouri History Museum, St Louis

Official Territorial Papers, 1800- 1815, National Archives, Washington, D.C.

Firearms, Traps, and Tools of the Mountain Men, by Carl P. Russel, Published by Skyhorse Publishing, Inc, 2011

William Clark Indian Diplomat, by Jay H. Buckley, Published by University of Oklahoma Press, 2008

Fur, Fortune, and Empire, by Eric Jay Dolin, Published by W.W. Norton & Company, New York and London, 2010

Three Years Among the Indians and Mexicans, by Thomas James, Edited by Walter B. Douglas, Published by the Missouri Historical Society, 1916

Undaunted Courage, by Stephen E. Ambrose, Published by Simon & Schuster, New York London Toronto Sydney, 1996

The Fate of the Corps, by Larry Morris, Published by Yale University Press, New Haven & London, 2004

Gloomy Terrors and Hidden Fires, by Ronald M. Anglin and Larry E. Morris, Published by Rowman and Littlefield, 2014

The Mystery of John Colter, by Ronald M. Anglin and Larry E. Morris, Published by Rowman & Littlefield, 2014

Blackfeet and Buffalo, by James Willard Schultz(Apikuni), Edited by Keith C. Seele, Published by University of Oklahoma Press, Norman, 1962

American Indian Life, Edited by Elsie Clews Parsons, Published by University of Nebraska Press, Lincoln, 1922

John Colter: His Years in the Rockies, by Burton Harris, Published by the University of Nebraska, Lincoln London, 1993